ONE HOUR OF FERVOR

ALSO BY

MURIEL BARBERY

The Elegance of the Hedgehog
Gourmet Rhapsody
The Life of Elves
A Strange Country
A Single Rose
The Writer's Cats

Muriel Barbery

ONE HOUR OF FERVOR

*Translated from the French
by Alison Anderson*

Europa
editions

Europa Editions
27 Union Square West, Suite 302
New York NY 10003
www.europaeditions.com
info@europaeditions.com

Copyright © Actes Sud 2022.
Published by special arrangement with Actes Sud
in conjunction with their appointed agent 2 Seas Literary Agency.
First Publication 2024 by Europa Editions

Translation by Alison Anderson
Original title: *Une heure de ferveur*
Translation copyright © 2024 by Europa Editions

Library of Congress Cataloging in Publication Data is available
ISBN 979-8-88966-004-0

Barbery, Muriel
One Hour of Fervor

Cover illustration by Hashimoto Kansetsu, *Soirée d'été* (detail), 1941

Cover design by Ginevra Rapisardi

Prepress by Grafica Punto Print – Rome

Printed in Canada

CONTENTS

to Chevalier

to all those from Kyōto
Akiyo, Megumi, Sayoko ✗
Keisuke, Manabu, Shigenori, Tomoo
Kazu, Tomoko

and Éric-Maria

ONE HOUR OF FERVOR

DYING

As he lay dying, Haru Ueno was looking at a flower and thinking, It's all been about a flower. There were, in fact, three threads to the narrative of his life, and only the last one was a flower. Stretching before him was a small temple garden that sought to be a miniature landscape, scattered with symbols. It was a wonder to him that centuries of spiritual seeking had ended in this precise arrangement—so much striving for meaning and, in the end, pure form, he thought, too.

For Haru Ueno was a seeker of form.

He knew he was about to die, and he thought, At last I'm in accordance with things. The gong at the Hōnen-in sounded in the distance, four times, and he felt so intensely alive to the world that it made him dizzy. There before him, the garden enclosed by white-washed walls topped with gray tiles. In the garden, three stones, a pine tree, an expanse of sand, a lantern, some moss. In the distance, the mountains of the East. The temple itself was known as the Shinnyo-dō. Every week for almost five decades Haru Ueno had taken a walk around the same loop: he went to the main temple on the hill, through the cemetery below it, and back to the entrance to the complex, where he was an important benefactor.

For Haru Ueno was a very rich man.

He had grown up watching the snow fall and melt on the stones of a mountain torrent. The little family house stood firmly on one bank. On the other was a forest of tall pine trees in the ice. He had long believed it was matter he loved—rock, water, leaves, and wood. Once he understood it was the form this matter took that he loved, he became an art dealer.

Art: one of the three threads of his life.

Of course, he didn't become an art dealer overnight. It had taken time to move to another city and meet a man. At the age of twenty, he had turned his back on the mountains and his father's sake business, and left Takayama for Kyōto. He had neither money nor connections, but he possessed a rare piece of good fortune: while he knew nothing of the world, he knew who he was. It was the month of May, and, seated on the wooden floor, he caught a glimpse of the future with a clarity that was close to the lucidity sake gives. All around, he could hear the bustle of the complex of Zen temples, where a cousin who was a monk had arranged a room for him. The encounter between the force of his vision and the immensity of time made his head spin. This vision did not say where, or when, or how. It said: A life devoted to art. And: I shall succeed. The room looked out on a tiny shady garden. In the distance, the sun gilded the stalks of tall gray bamboo. Water irises grew among the hostas and dwarf ferns. One of the irises, taller and more slender than the others, was swaying in the breeze. Somewhere a bell was tolling. Time contracted, and Haru Ueno was that flower. Then the moment passed.

On this day, fifty years later, Haru Ueno gazed at the same flower and was astonished that once again it was the twentieth of May at four o'clock in the afternoon. One thing, however, was different: this time, he was looking at the flower in himself.

Another element was the same: everything—the iris, the bell, the garden—was there in the present. A final observation was remarkable: in this total present, the pain faded away. He heard a sound behind him and hoped he would be left alone. He thought of Keisuke, who was waiting somewhere for him to die, and told himself, A life can be summed up in three names.

Haru, who did not want to die. Keisuke, who could not die. Rose, who would live.

The private quarters where he was lying were those of the temple's head monk, who was the twin brother of Keisuke Shibata, thanks to whom he'd found his vocation. The Shibata brothers descended from an old Kyōto family who, for as long as anyone could remember, had provided the city with monks and lacquerers. Since Keisuke despised both religion and—because of its shine—lacquer, he had opted for pottery, but he was also a painter, calligrapher, and poet. What was remarkable about Haru and Keisuke's encounter was that, at the very beginning, there had been a bowl between them. Haru saw this bowl and knew what his life would be. He'd never come across such a work of art: the bowl seemed both new and very old, in a way that he'd thought was *impossible*. Next to it, sprawled on a chair, was a man of indeterminate age and—could this make sense?— of the same alloy as the bowl. On top of it, he was dead drunk, and Haru found himself confronted with an equation that was equally impossible: on the one hand, perfect form, and on the other, its creator: a drunkard. Once they'd been introduced, they placed the seal, with sake, on what would become the friendship of a lifetime.

Friendship: the second narrative thread in Haru's life.

And now death stood before him in the guise of a garden, and all the rest, with the exception of those two instants a half-century apart, had become invisible. A cloud touched the summit of Daimon-ji and left the scent of iris in its wake. Haru thought, All that remains are these two moments, and Rose.

Rose, the third thread.

BEFORE

H aru Ueno and Keisuke Shibata had met fifty years earlier at the home of Tomoo Hasegawa, who produced
art documentaries for national television. Although
the Japanese, as a rule, rarely entertain at home, at Tomoo's
you could meet both Japanese and foreign artists, and all sorts
of people who weren't artists. The place looked like a sailing
ship beached on a mossy shore. On the upper deck, the wind
came in through the windows, even in the depths of winter.
The rear of the vessel clung to a flank of the Shinnyo-dō. The
prow faced the mountains of the East. Tomoo had designed it
and had it built in the early 1960s, then kept an open house for
anyone who was hungry for art, sake, and partying. The partying included friendship and laughter late into the night. The art
and the sake were pure. They kept forever, just as they were.
Nothing ever came to alter their essence.

And so, for almost ten years, Tomoo Hasegawa had reigned
from his hillside. People called him Hasegawa-san or Tochan,
the latter an affectionate diminutive reserved for children.
People came and went at all hours, regardless of whether he
was there. They loved him. They wished they could be like
him, but no one held this against him. Beyond that, he adored
Keisuke, Keisuke adored him, and, almost as if it were meant
to be, they both enjoyed the cold. No matter the season, they
would wander along the paths of the temple half-dressed, and,
on January 10, 1970, at dawn, Haru joined them for the first

time. In the pale light the hill was like an ice field, its stone lanterns glowing and the air redolent of flint and incense. The other two were chirping away in their thin garments, but Haru, who was wearing a thick coat, found himself shivering. Yet he didn't mind, and in this glacial dawn he came to see he was a pilgrim. His family home was in Takayama, but the place where he had lived and would live his true life was Shinnyo-dō. Haru didn't believe in past lives, but he did believe in the spirit. Henceforth, he would be a pilgrim. Forever returning to his true origins.

The Shinnyo-dō: a temple adjacent to other temples, perched on a hill in the northeast of the city; by extension, Haru referred to the hill by the same name. There were maple trees everywhere, old buildings, a wooden pagoda, stone walkways. And, naturally, set on the summit and sides of the hill, there were cemeteries, including those of Shinnyo-dō and Kurodani, to which Haru, once he had money, would give with equal generosity. Every week for nearly fifty years he would go through the red gate and climb up to the temple, go around it, and continue south along the side of two cemeteries and through a third one, gaze out at Kyōto below him, head down Kurodani's stone stairway, and wind his way northward between the temples until he reached his starting point. And, at every instant, he would know this was his home. Since he was only a Buddhist out of respect for tradition but wanted to join everything in his life together, he had forged the conviction that Buddhism was the name his culture had given to art, or, at the very least, to that root of art called the spirit. The spirit embraced everything, explained everything. For some mysterious reason, the hill of Shinnyo-dō incarnated the essence of that spirit. When Haru went for his circular walk, he was going through life, the bare bones of it, stripped of all obscenity, cleansed of triviality. Over the years, he'd come to realize that these enlightened understandings were born of the configuration of the place itself. Over the centuries, man had brought together buildings and gardens, had laid out the temples, trees, and lanterns, and, in the end, this patient labor had given rise to a miracle: to stride along the walkway was to converse intimately with the invisible. Many people attributed this to the higher presences that haunt sacred places, but Haru had learned from the stones of his torrent that spirit arises from form, that there is only form, the grace or disgrace resulting from it—eternity or death contained in the curves of a rock. And so, during that winter of 1970 when he was still a nobody, he decided that one day his ashes would be buried in that place. For Haru Ueno knew not only who he was, he knew what he wanted. He was only waiting to understand the form it would take.

Consequently, when he made the acquaintance of Keisuke Shibata, he saw his future as clearly as an earthenware bowl in broad daylight. That evening, Tomoo Hasegawa, playing patron of the arts, was holding a launch party at his home for a handful of atypical young artists. As was customary, they brought their work to the Shinnyo-dō sailing ship, and then everyone who was anyone in Kyōto came, drank, and chatted before they left again to spread the artists' names. Most of these artists were free spirits. They did not belong to a school or a family. They sought to be—a culturally complicated thing—*exceptional*. They didn't copy contemporary Western art. They worked the clay of their native land, giving it a totally new cast that always looked Japanese, without belonging to any artistic lineage. In fact, these artists were very much to Haru's taste, because they resembled the individual he himself would like to be: young, yet deep; loyal, yet free of any bonds; thoughtful, yet full of audacity.

In those days, the few galleries dealing in contemporary art only survived by selling traditional work, as well, which was a very exclusive market requiring an entrée. Haru, the son of a modest sake brewer from the mountains, had no hope of getting his foot in the door. He paid for his room at the Daitoku-ji by helping out with the temple's maintenance tasks, and for his studies in architecture and English by working evenings at a bar. His entire worldly possessions consisted of a bicycle, a few books, and the tea service his grandfather had given him. Finally, the fourth thing he owned was a coat, which he wore from November to May, indoors and out, suffering as he did from the cold. And yet, even if he had nothing, back in that glacial January, a magnificent compass had just been placed in his bare hands. He said to himself, I'll do the same thing as Tomoo, but on a grander scale.

And he did. But first, after a certain number of other sake-filled nights, he described his project to Keisuke and declared, I need your money to get started. In the guise of an answer, Keisuke told him a story. In around 1600, the son of a merchant wanted to become a samurai, so his father said to him, I am old and have no other heirs, but samurai honor the way of tea, and, for that reason, I will give you my blessing. The next day, Haru invited Keisuke into his room, and with his grandfather's tea service, he prepared tea for him, performing a casual yet nevertheless somewhat solemn ceremony. Then they drank sake and conversed, laughing all the while. The snow falling on the temples covered the curving roofs of the lanterns with immaculate ravens' wings, and then, without warning, Keisuke launched into a tirade on the inanity of religion. Buddhism is not a religion, said Haru, or else it's the religion of art. In that case, it's also the religion of sake, Keisuke asserted. Haru agreed, and they drank some more. In the end, he specified the amount he would need, and Keisuke lent him the money.

Subsequently Haru would excel at circumventing obstacles. He had no premises for his gallery, he rented a warehouse. He had no network, he used Tomoo's. He had no reputation, he went about making other people's. He charmed everyone, and Keisuke's assumption proved correct: deep down, Haru was a tradesman, but unlike his father, he would be a great tradesman, because he had a good instinct not only for business but also for tea—or, to put it differently, for grace. The fact is, there are two sorts of grace. The first is that which results from a spirit that is born of form, and, for that, Haru went to Shinnyo-dō. The second is merely the first seen from a different angle, but because it takes on a specific appearance, it's called beauty. For that type of grace, Haru went to Zen gardens and spent time with artists. His tea eye probed their works and broke through to the soul of each one, something he summed up by saying, I don't have talent, but I do have taste. But he was wrong about that, because there is also a third sort of grace, in which the other two are steeped, and in this, Keisuke saw supreme talent. And even if, in Haru's case, it was rooted in a paradox, it was no less powerful: his whole life long, he would fail at love, but when it came to friendship, he would be a master.

F riendship: and yet, it is a part of love.

One day, after Haru had dwelled at length on his predilection for Western women, Keisuke said, "For me, everything—life, art, the soul, woman—has been drawn with the same ink."

"Which ink is that?" asked Haru.

"Japan," said Keisuke. "I can't imagine touching a foreign woman."

For Haru, that was inconceivable, even though he understood Keisuke's love for his wife. And to be honest, who would not? Sae Shibata was everything a heart could desire. When you met her, you felt a spear lodge in your heart. It didn't hurt but, instead, was like watching the slow unwinding of an ineffable act. What sort of act? You didn't know, you actually didn't know much at all—was she beautiful, petite, lively or serious, no one could have said. Pale, yes. But otherwise, nothing lingered, just an intense presence with whom you'd come a long way. And then one November evening in 1975, on a coast road near Kaseda, where their mother and grandmother lived, an earthquake brought down a tree, and Sae and little Yōko with it. A slight trembling of the earth—then all was gone. The tree falls on the car, and infinity dies.

"It's just the beginning," Keisuke told Haru.

"There's no reason it should continue," Haru assured him.

"Cut the crap," said Keisuke.

"All right," Haru replied.

And he was by the potter's side, with no useless words, when ten years later, on February 14, 1985, Tarō, Keisuke's eldest son, died, and again twenty-six years later, on March 11, 2011, when it was the turn of Nobu, his youngest son.

"But I cannot die," said Keisuke, after Tarō's death. "It's called fate," he explained, reaching for the cup of sake Haru held out to him.

"How do you know that?" asked Haru.

"The stars," said Keisuke. "If only you knew how to listen. But you don't know how to listen—mountain folk are real dumbasses."

In fact, if anything, Haru Ueno was blunt, the way mountain folk sometimes are, and in a little less than ten years, he had succeeded beyond all expectation. He had stuck to his early habit of renting ephemeral spaces to exhibit his artists. The only thing he had bought was a warehouse. In other aspects, everything had changed: he was rich, he was powerful, his artists were praised to the skies. There were various reasons for this, including his knowing when to seize a market opportunity. And once he was well-positioned, he was not only clever at finding his protégés but also chose his buyers with an equal mixture of sincerity and calculation. It was hard to imagine how much this kindled desire: not only did people want the art, they also wanted to be Haru Ueno's clients. In the beginning, he officiated on his own, although Keisuke was often hanging around, off in some corner while a sale was being finalized. There was always sake on hand, and they would drink until late in the evening, when Haru took everyone out for dinner somewhere. Once the others had been drunk under the table, Keisuke and Haru walked home in the moonlight. In those deep hours, they spoke about things that mattered. Why do you drink? Haru would ask, long before his friend's wife had died. Because I know my fate, said Keisuke. And when Sae and little Yōko died he said to Haru, I told you so. Another time, Haru said, Which would you keep, the invisible or the sublime? Keisuke didn't come by for several days, but when he did, he brought Haru the most beautiful picture he'd ever painted. Sometimes they simply stood in wonder gazing at the stars, smoking and talking about art. At other times, Keisuke told stories that were equally threaded with classical literature and personal lore. Finally they would say good night and go their separate ways, their homes only a stone's throw from each other on the banks of the Kamo-gawa.

The Kamo-gawa: the metronome of Haru's life was his weekly walk to Shinnyo-dō, but his anchor was set by the banks of the river that runs north to south through Kyōto, slicing it into two distinct entities. All the locals know as much: it is on its banks, along its sandy pathways, among the wild grasses and herons that the pulse of the old city can be felt. Give me water and a mountain, said Keisuke, and I'll make the world for you, the valley where the unfathomable winds its way. Haru bought an old riverside ruin that turned its back on the west and faced the mountains of the East. He had not yet finished his architecture studies, but God knew he could draw a house. In place of the crumbling dwelling he built a marvel of glass and wood. Outside, it gave onto the water and the mountains. Inside, it opened onto tiny gardens. In the middle of the main room, in a glass cage open to the sky, there lived a young maple tree. Haru's furniture was sparse and tasteful, and he brought in a few art works. For his bedroom he sought total asceticism, his only concessions a futon and Keisuke's painting. In the morning he drank his tea while gazing at the joggers along the riverside with its maple and cherry trees. In the evening he worked alone in a study with slanting bay windows that faced the mountains of the East and the North. Then finally he would go to bed, after another day spent in the valley of the unfathomable. Half of the time, however, he was not alone: at the warehouse, he threw parties, with dancing and drinking among the storage chests; at home, he hosted friendly gatherings, with drinking and conversation by the maple tree cage. People went just as often to Tomoo's place—where Haru was sure to be found— as to Haru's, where Tomoo was always welcome. Keisuke was there on every occasion.

January 20, 1979. Of course Keisuke is there. Sae and Yōko have already died, but Tarō and Nobu, his two sons, are still alive. In their company, in the newly unveiled house by the Kamo-gawa, Haru is celebrating his thirtieth birthday. As usual, there are the regular guests, a few strangers, and a great many women. Sake is being served, there is light-hearted laughter, time resembles a palm leaf caressed by the breeze. Outside, it is snowing, and in the maple tree cage, the stone lantern is wearing its immaculate ravens' wings. A woman comes in with Tomoo, and Haru sees her from behind, sees her ginger hair coiled in a loose chignon, her green dress, the gems at her ears. She is speaking with Tomoo. She observes the maple tree, turns around, and he sees her face for the first time. Then, all at once, like the fog that sometimes steals in without warning, that was the end of light-heartedness.

Y ou cannot fan away the fog," Keisuke is saying to a young sculptor, not looking at him, because it's Haru he's looking at.

He falls silent, and after a moment, the young sculptor, puzzled, slips away, mumbling an excuse, but Keisuke, absorbed by the fire that is spreading, pays no attention to him. He knows how to see the stars, and he knows fires—so he has no doubt: this woman has a fire inside her. He's not afraid for Haru, not yet. He's afraid for her. He has never met anyone who was such a *non-presence*.

"This is Maud; she's French," says Tomoo, and Keisuke thinks, The fog.

Haru is next to them, and Keisuke thinks, The fan. He meets the Frenchwoman's gaze, with those green eyes and their elegant shadows. She says something in English, and Haru makes a comment, with a few words and a laugh.

"I don't speak English," says Keisuke in Japanese.

She gives a wave of her hand that might mean either, It doesn't matter, or Who cares. They all have the feeling that space, or perhaps, time, has been distorted, then things return to what, apparently, is normal, and Keisuke knows she will spend the night at Haru's. There are several women in the room tonight who are, or have been, his mistresses. Haru is the most charming of men and the best of friends, for whom love branches out from friendship and the branch of family is too low down—before Sae and Yōko died, he was in the habit of saying, You bump your head, I prefer the higher branches. At the funeral, as friendship is a part of love, he said, Fate is no good at choosing branches.

That evening, however, that very same Haru tries to dispel the fog. With a cup of sake in his hand, deprived of visibility, he flutters his fans, that of his conversation in perfect English, the envy of all the Japanese, and that of humor, which he deploys in a bantering European manner that he owes in particular to the time he's spent with the French. But nothing dispels the mystery. She tells him she's the press attaché at a cultural institute, so he ventures a lesson in Japanese art. She listens, impassive, and at one point, she murmurs, *I agree*, the way you might say, *I am dying*. Haru is lost in this woman. She seems infinite to him, and, at the same time, she isn't there. He finds himself facing a void inhabited by dead stars. He notices that she has a beautiful mouth, its corners curled into a comely fold, and he senses that he will get what he wants and, at the same time, that there's something he cannot grasp.

At the far end of the room, something is alarming Keisuke, although he cannot see exactly what it is, and so, because sake is a torch placed at the root of things, he drinks. An hour later, the only clear result is that he's dead drunk, sitting on the floor, his back against the maple tree cage, his legs stretched out, his head crowned and backlit with glittering ravens' wings. It's a beautiful night, lacquered with snow. The sky has iced over, the stars light the ink of it without shining. Haru and the Frenchwoman are on the other side of the tree, and once again Keisuke is struck by a hollowness about her that leaves the sake powerless, since evanescence has no roots. And yet this non-presence, these fluid, indifferent gestures give off a scent of something burning. He is aware of her emerald-green dress, the gems at her ears, her lipstick, her fine features. Everything else is undefined—proportions, articulations, cohesion, the way the whole is put together. Keisuke cannot imagine this woman as a whole, and he knows that this is not the effect of alcohol but of the absence, in her, of those invisible joints that connect the scattered fragments of a human being. He is overwhelmed by the memory of Sae: they are in the house by the Kamo-gawa, he recognizes the room, the light, his wife's body, and in the fluid fire that is Maud, he can see her opposite. To be honest, he cannot make out either form or contour, and he feels as if he has been afflicted by a certain blindness, but this inability to grasp the usual parameters of vision is what gives him this unprecedented discernment. In this way, he sees through the mist to where what is visible is hidden and what is invisible is revealed. He is sworn, forever, to his widowed state and to art, the only territory where he can still create presences. Sometimes, after a great deal of sake, friendship adds its own presences, and of all its clan, Haru shines brightest in the dark. There is something *incarnate* about that mountain yokel, although Keisuke detects in him some endearing marks of cracking. As for all the rest, art in particular, they find themselves on different ranges of the spectrum: Haru is eager for form, which Keisuke seeks to erase: he hunts for the invisible in hiding places where neither features, nor texture, nor colors exist. All are erased so that the naked thing—no longer thing, but presence—might be grasped, and in this blindfolded race, Keisuke always hopes to see spirit itself.

"But in the end, it's either a woman or a bowl," Haru says.

"You're blind, because you only look," Keisuke replies. "You must learn not to look."

So there is Keisuke, sprawled against the maple tree cage, his gaze calibrated by the scale Sae left him. He is terrified by the fire that Maud has lit, and thinks, What does it do, a fire burning in a vacuum? It doesn't rise higher, it doesn't flare up, it slowly consumes itself. And as his vision grows sharper, the certainty that he is missing something intensifies; he finds it strange to be there so close to the heart of tragedy without being able to see it. Alas, he's too drunk to interpret the scene, and he looks at Haru, who is wittering on while she listens, dreamily, her head tilted slightly to one side. Haru is not aware that Keisuke is watching him. He is very intoxicated, not with alcohol but with the favor of this foreign woman. She surprises and enchants him, he is besotted with her profile, fit for a cameo, her light complexion, her ginger hair. Confusedly, beyond that—beyond what?—he sees another oddity, decides he will examine it *after*. All he wants is to kiss that mouth, caress those shoulders and breasts, penetrate that body, and he thinks, The rest will be revealed *after*.

W hen, forty years later, Haru Ueno contemplates death dressed as a garden, he sees their lives again, sculpted by what came after: after Sae, after Maud, after Rose—and he thinks, Keisuke wore himself out telling me this, and I ignored all the signs, I saw none of it because I kept on looking. But on January 20, 1979, the guests gradually leave the house. They roll Keisuke out in a wheelbarrow and laugh into the night, because the cold doesn't frighten voyagers from before. One of them, however, knows that they've already tipped into after, that henceforth there will be nothing but a long litany of afters, that life is nothing but one neverending after. While he was settling Keisuke in his wheelbarrow, Tomoo, drunk as a lord, said to him, *Haru*, but Keisuke heard *danger*. For those who have an inner eye, sake is pure. Nothing, ever, can alter its essence. Keisuke thinks it'll have their hides, but it won't have their souls. With the naked eye and the help of sake, they have seen that Haru is in danger.

In the deserted house by the Kamo-gawa, Haru slips into the water, and the Frenchwoman steps in after him. He talks to her about hinoki wood and his nostalgia for *sentō* and an era when the Japanese did not yet have baths at home. She is sitting across from him, running her hand over the smooth wooden edge of the bath.

"But *sentō* still exist," she murmurs.

He nods. "They will disappear."

The large bath shimmers in the half-light of the late hour. The moon and the lanterns of the inner garden illuminate her face and body. Her breasts are white, she has the shoulders of a ballerina, she's slender, like a reed, delicately thin. For some unknown reason, Haru thinks of a story Keisuke told him, and he opens this new fan.

"In around the middle of the Heian period, in the year one thousand of your calendar," he says, "the dawns were stunningly beautiful. In the depths of the heavens, sprays of purple flowers were withering. Sometimes huge birds were caught in this burning light. At the imperial court there lived a lady, confined to her quarters. Her nobility had sealed her fate as a captive, and even the little garden adjacent to her room was forbidden to her. But to contemplate the dawn, she knelt on the wood of the outside veranda, and every morning since the New Year, a fox cub had stolen into the garden."

Haru falls silent.

"And?" says the Frenchwoman.

"A heavy rain began to fall, lasting until the spring, and the lady begged her new friend to come and shelter with her under the roof of the veranda by the garden, where there were only a few winter camellias and a maple tree. There, they became acquainted, in silence, but then, once they'd invented a shared language, to each other they said only the names of their dead."

Haru falls silent, and this time, she doesn't say anything. When he thinks he has seen someone moving through the mist, it seems to him as if a fortress is growing, a fortress of shadows, immense and impregnable, and he is overcome by an equally immense desire to possess this woman. Later still, he marvels at the miracle of those open thighs, that sex he has penetrated. He is transported by her body, something indefinable that troubles him all the while, amplifying his desire. She is staring at the large painting opposite the bed, and sometimes she makes a faint gesture that is powerfully erotic to him. Immediately afterward, he drifts off into a chaos of dreams, where the fox and the bath visit in turns. The woman flows between his fingers, a prisoner, but liquid, and, above all, she is *elsewhere*.

When he awakes, he is alone. On the nights that follow, she comes again. In the bath, he tells her a story. After that, they go to the bedroom. Each time, she stares at the painting. To Haru, her body's a source of endless wonder. He feels himself entering a crystal-clear stream, and, in this total lack of resistance he sees a total gift. He is helplessly lost to her hips, her skin, her rare gestures, and he has lost all his certainties, all his bearings. If women are drawn to Haru, it's because he loves their pleasure, but with her, he doesn't give it a second thought. He has crossed a border and accepted the customs of a strange country; he imagines that her pleasure—it, too—is *elsewhere*. A few days from then he will think that he has taken indifference for consent, the abyss for passion, and then: that he wanted this abyss. But that night, the tenth, he stretches himself over that ghost woman and enters her the way one slices through a black wave. Earlier that evening, they met at Tomoo's place, and all he could think of was the moment he would embrace that pale body. At one point, to arrange a lock of hair, she used a gesture she had made during lovemaking, and for the first time in his life as a man he wanted a woman—this woman—for himself alone. He doesn't think about the fact that in ten nights she has not addressed ten words to him. In the fog, he doesn't see the fire. He sees green eyes and the movements of a dancer. As always, he is looking at form.

He penetrates her, and her silent passivity leads him into moments of unprecedented ecstasy. Probably, if she came to life, the spell would be broken, but she does not come to life, and he loses himself in his own delight. He comes and goes in this fissure of light, anything this woman might want, he will want, too. Then, suddenly, something shifts, and she is someone else to him. In the breaking dawn, her naked body is diaphanous, and, for the first time, she's not staring at the painting: she's observing it. Her pupils are dilated, her eyes dark; he is terror-stricken to feel that he's pinning an insect alive. Her pallor is a trap where light is absorbed, and he climaxes silently, held by a sensation of disaster. She gets up, gets dressed, tells him she's going to Tōkyō, that she'll see him again when she gets back. He doesn't understand, but he has no doubt, either: this is the end, and he doesn't even know what of.

AFTER

A nd so, Haru Ueno was born and would die looking at an iris. Now he knew: to be aware of things, he had to be born or to die, and every time, this would happen in a garden.

The Daitoku-ji Zen of his youth abounded in beauty, the likes of which he had found nowhere else. In these timeless waters, side by side, there were camellias, maples, bamboo, lanterns, sand, and wooden buildings sculpted like lace, scattered with secret lattices and enchanting niches. At Shinnyo-dō, on the other hand, the temple was dark and massive, as if offering protection from a storm. The same austerity meant that the head monk's private garden contained only three stones, a pine tree, a strip of gray sand and a lantern embedded in the moss, but, according to time-honored tradition, the scenery directed one's gaze to the more expansive landscape of the mountains of the East. I have so loved these nuptials between what is closed and what is open, thought Haru, and yet now all I want are these three stones and this sand raked with waves. He thought back to one of Keisuke's favorite stories: in the China of old, an emperor thanks a wise counsellor by asking him to choose a gift from among his infinite riches, and when all the counsellor asks for is a bowl of rice and a cup of tea, they chop off his head in response, on the grounds of impertinence. Whenever he told the story, Keisuke would laugh, and now Haru thought, He told me this story for the day I die. I'm holding the world in my hands, and I have chosen an iris and a rose. Soon, the price of this treasure will be my head. Behind him, the sound of a door sliding, and he closed his eyes. I've brought you this from Keisuke, said Paul's voice. When he was alone again, Haru opened his eyes and saw a black bowl set before him. He thought, Of course, everything was done, and undone, at Tomoo's place.

In fact, ever since that first dawn, Haru had understood: Shinnyo-dō was a land of pilgrimage; Tomoo was the guardian, Keisuke the ferryman. The monks believe that only the dead cross the last river, but Haru was convinced that Keisuke had crossed back and forth multiple times in his life, and that the place where that river flowed was Shinnyo-dō. One day, he too would cross it in the boat of friendship, and perhaps he in turn would see the world according to Keisuke. Although he did not associate with death, he had always felt at home there on the hill because he believed in the truth of the river, the invisible turned visible, and tea. Now, five decades after he first came upon Keisuke's bowl at Tomoo's, he could truly see it for the first time. The bowl was fading but hadn't disappeared, it was matte, simple, bare. Haru gazed at it, and before long, its form vanished, leaving only an imprint without substance or contour, and this brought deep tranquility. Haru thought, At last I've broken through the fog.

After a week, the Frenchwoman came back from Tōkyō, and he saw her again at Tomoo's place. Her expression, when she saw him, was hostile, and he'd turned away from her. He no longer desired her; her coldness was reptilian, he was just waiting for her to leave so his life could go back to normal. Keisuke hadn't shown up, and Haru left early, went home, took a bath, read for a while and went to bed. He wasn't afraid of suffering, even though he knew that somewhere—in him, in her—a vestige of those ten strange nights would remain. But over time, an exquisite time of women and walking in the snow, he began to feel a faint disquiet. As if Maud's trace were touching him lightly in a blind spot buried deep inside him. If he thought of those ten days with her, he was incapable of *picturing* them. Everything was located in a dead angle, and he was both blind and aware of his sightlessness. Though he thought he knew himself, he could no longer see himself properly, and the more he went on with his life from before (insidiously, doubting it had really become that life again), the more his disquiet grew. When he was making love—when he reconnected with the joy of making love to a woman—he didn't think about Maud, but he felt a new apprehension about himself, as if an infinitesimal shift had blurred the finely calibrated map of his being. What was more, his initial disquiet had been followed by a diffuse sentiment of something menacing.

At a party at Tomoo's, the last one before the Frenchwoman left Japan, Haru met an English woman. He already knew her husband, a property developer from Tōkyō who had just moved his wife and son to Kyōto. Haru didn't like the man, nor did he have any respect for tradesmen who only cared about money. In the Haru System, money was there to realize the way of art, to acquire sake, and to build glass cages for maple trees. Beth, the developer's wife, was cut from the same cloth. They were introduced, they chatted for a few minutes about trivial things, and he knew that he would sleep with her and that they would be great friends. She was a hard woman, but her hardness was of a kind that couldn't hurt him, because she expected others to know where they lived, within themselves and in the world, and if they didn't, she would be on her way. Like Haru, she despised money; like him, she loved being in charge and building things, though in those days she'd been excluded from taking part in the family firm. Upon her husband's death, she would turn that business into an empire. After lovemaking, Haru liked to see her sitting before him, naked, blonde, and angular, drinking a cup of tea while they talked about their respective affairs. He knew she had other lovers, that her husband didn't mind, that she lived in unimaginable licentiousness, all in a country where men and women were unaccustomed to women being free. Finally, she had a ten-year-old son, William, the only person she would ever love and whom, through her own fault, she would lose. When she talked about him, her skin took on a pearly sheen, her eyes went dark, and she was extraordinarily beautiful, illuminated by the transports of love. Fate enjoys bleeding us dry, depriving us of the very things that keep us on our feet, and for those who can stare at fate without flinching, it responds by reinforcing its punishment. On May 20, 2019, four decades later, Haru saw Beth and Maud bathed in a new clarity, and he thought, This is how the puzzle pieces fit together: I thought I loved their hardness, but what I saw was their strangeness— their strangeness, their solitude, their wounds, and my own.

On that evening in the spring of 1979, Haru and Beth become lovers, and when he kisses those Western lips, melts into that Western body, he feels that at last Maud has withdrawn from him. So, since fate always increases its ire against those who look at it without flinching, it will come back to knock at the door of the house by the Kamo-gawa.

The woman who opens the door is called Sayoko. As for the messenger from fate, he looks every bit like an impeccably dressed forty-year-old, stationed beneath a transparent umbrella with an object wrapped in silk tucked under his arm. His name is Jacques Melland, he works in Paris as an antique dealer, specialized in Asian art, and he has two passions: Siamese cats and Kyōto. He also happens to have a wife, three sons, and difficulty understanding why life causes human beings to be born in the wrong place and the wrong body. When, the day before, he met Haru Ueno at Tomoo Hasegawa's place, Jacques knew at once: this was the man he would have liked to be. Now that he's seeing his home, regret turns to pain.

Sayoko looks at him. He clears his throat. He is awed by Japanese women in kimonos, never quite sure he can measure up to their exceptional clan. Moreover, he doesn't know whether she's Haru's wife, sister, mistress, or housekeeper. The day before, the art dealer merely told him to come by before dinner. Jacques Melland is dressed to the nines, as if he were off to a romantic rendezvous, and now he has forgotten why he is here—he has even forgotten that he speaks Japanese, and he hears the woman asking him in a voice with a broken intonation, "Melland-san?"

He nods his head, and she adds, "Ueno-san wait for you inside."

In the vestibule, branches of magnolia are taking flight from a large vase with dark sides. In the room where Haru is waiting for him, there is a maple tree in a glass cage. Jacques Melland is overcome with disgust at the thought of his apartment in Paris's eighth arrondissement, a long succession of rooms with a *point de Hongrie* parquet floor. This sort of disgust visits him often in Kyōto, but, this time, not only does he want to live in this place, he also wants to become this man. It makes him lose the thread of the story he likes to tell about himself—elegance, savoir-faire, and *Grand Siècle* curtains—and he thinks, I would give ten years of my life for this man's. "Oh, hello, hello," says the art dealer in English, motioning for him to join him by the low table where he's sitting. The Japanese woman stays there for a moment, her hands folded over her orange obi, until she slips away, taking tiny, muffled steps. She comes back carrying a tray with a sake service decorated with cherry blossoms. The liquid Haru pours is whitish in hue, slightly sparkling, and a little cloudy.

"It's from Takayama," says his Japanese host. "My father and brother have a small business there."

"How did you make your fortune?" asks Jacques, and Haru laughs.

"I found my home," he replies.

Jacques looks around him.

"No, no," says Haru, "not this one, but if you have time tomorrow, I'll take you there."

The Frenchman says that he does have time, then remembers why he has come and places on the table the silk-wrapped form he has brought from the hotel. He knows that Haru will not open it in front of him, and so he says, "I always bring one with me and give it to whoever opens a door for me."

"Not the door of fortune, I suppose," says Haru.

"No," says Jacques, "an invisible door."

They drink for a while longer in silence, then Jacques stands up and Haru says, "I'll come for you tomorrow at your hotel at half past three."

The next day at half past three, Jacques Melland stands waiting outside the hotel entrance. He is wearing the ascot he saves for special occasions, red with white polka dots, and he knows he's on the verge of secret nuptials. In the taxi, Haru tells him a story about a fox, a story he'll remember one day— the day of his death—but for the time being, he listens without understanding why. At last the car stops outside a lane leading to a high red gate. A few cherry petals flutter in the warm May breeze, and beyond the gate Melland can see stone steps, flanked by lanterns and maple trees, leading up to a low temple. On the right is a wooden pagoda, before the temple is a vast courtyard, all around there are annexes. The place is deserted, and if Jacques Melland, with his silk ascots, his cashmere dressing gowns and dinners at his club, still harbored any doubt, it has just been swept away, because, here, there is a plethora of invisible doors. The Frenchman follows the Japanese man to the entrance of the temple, and, absorbed by his inner turmoil, he hears nothing. With awestruck reverence, he steps over unknown thresholds and feels a presence behind him, but when he turns around, there's not a soul. He wonders how he missed this place, when he often goes just over the way, to the Silver Pavilion, and regularly visits the shrine of Yoshida, a stone's throw from there. Unfortunately, he knows the answer: he is not Haru Ueno, he is not Japanese, he is just poor Jacques Melland. The art dealer beckons to him to go around the temple, and they find themselves beneath the loveliest vault of maple trees in the galaxy, with foliage curved in an infinitely slender arc. It tears at his heart, and, lost in a happy torment, he doesn't hear what his companion has asked him. "I beg your pardon?" he murmurs, and Haru repeats his question: "Well, the invisible door?" And without waiting for an answer, he heads off to the right, along a path of stone and sand making its way between the cemeteries.

Somewhere in the distance, a gong sounds four times. Somewhere else, deep within Jacques Melland's secret territories, a connection is made, and the reality he is walking through, made of tombs and stone lanterns, is changing its *matter*. Everywhere, quivering in the breeze, there are thin wooden stalks bearing inscriptions, where he thinks he can read the text of his initiation. After a short stroll they reach the end of the lane and find themselves at the top of a grand flight of steps that cuts through the cemetery to other temples set in the hollow of the hill. Behind them is a wooden pagoda, below them is Kyōto, sprawling in its basin, beyond lie the mountains of the West. Time is dusted with a fine powder, spread over the paths of the world, transfiguring the hours, and between birth and death, Jacques Melland has ambled along the trajectory of life.

At the top of the steps, they pause and gaze out at the city.

"Rilke," says Melland, in answer to a question Haru asked him ten minutes earlier.

Haru looks at him.

"Yesterday, at Tomoo Hasegawa's place," says Melland, "we were admiring the mountains in their soft May greenery, and I said, It's lovely, but the most beautiful season is autumn. And then you quoted Rilke: 'The leaves fall, fall as from far / Like distant gardens withered in the heavens.'"

"Ah," says Haru, "I first heard those lines from my friend Keisuke. He's mad about Rilke."

"But that's exactly what it is, what Japan really is: heavens where gardens wither."

Haru smiles at him.

"Gardens for gods," Jacques adds. "You cannot imagine how important it is to me to have opened this door."

"Oh, believe me, I can," Haru says, "I know what it means, the life of a man."

They fall silent for a moment, then Jacques says, "What was that gong?"

"The gong at Hōnen-in," says Haru. "The monks ring it every day at closing time."

"The little temple south of the Silver Pavilion?"

Haru nods and points in that direction.

"We're at Kurodani, the common name for the temple of Konkaikōmyō-ji. Tochan lives on the eastern slope of Shinnyō-do, two minutes from here. The Silver Pavilion is a bit further away, a twenty-minute walk."

On either side of the steps there are walkways mixed with graves and heavenly bamboo. Melland knows that nothing happens by chance and that, from now on, his entire life will be contained in every instant of that interval separating Tochan's house from these steps in the cemetery. He might die an old man, and he's already lived a good life, but the essence of his existence is being distilled here and now, just this once and for eternity. He takes a deep breath, both of rebirth and grief. His happiness and desperation leave him on the verge of tears. This is it, he thinks, a life can amount to two days and a few hundred steps. His Japanese companion says nothing, but Melland, helplessly in love with this ferryman who has just made a pilgrim of him, wants to honor the destiny that has placed him in his path.

"It was a friend who told me to go to Tomoo's place, and thanks to her, I met you. Her name is Maud Arden, do you know her?"

"Ah, Maud," says Haru, lightly, "how is she doing?"

"Oh," says Jacques, "I don't know. It's hard to tell with her."

He thinks of something else and then, for no reason, thinks again of Maud.

"In any event," he adds, "she's pregnant."

*

There's a silence that Melland doesn't notice, but Haru has completely forgotten the Frenchman's presence. A second ago he'd found himself growing fond of this tradesman turned man of faith. Now he's thinking that his tomb will be here, where he first learned of his daughter's existence. For he does not doubt that the child is his, nor does he doubt that it will be a girl. All at once he sees himself as a willing father—a father without a family, the father of a foreign child—and he is greatly moved by this, even as he continues to take it in. He doesn't know whether his life is no longer his own, or has never been more so. Someone has just flicked a switch, and a room in his own house that he didn't know existed has been flooded with light. He is both lost and dazzled, and he thinks: Maud was not an end but a beginning. The feeling of closeness—but with what?—is so strong that it enfolds his entire life. With the same terrifying clarity, he sees the clouds gathering in the far heavens. He decides to donate money to the temple, mentally composes a letter to Maud, and processes both the vertiginous transfer of his property to a creature yet unborn and the crystallization of his life into three words carved in the stone of Kurodani. He feels neither anger nor uncertainty, and he thinks, This thread cannot be broken. He listens distractedly to the Frenchman as they resume their stroll through the buildings in the complex, and he muses that they are two men who have been struck by revelation, finding their path through the avenues of the spirit.

"What's the name of your favorite son?" Haru asks.

"Naturally, I don't have a favorite son," Jacques replies, "but his name is Édouard. The other two are brutes. I think Édouard will be gay, and he'll take over the shop."

After that, they speak casually. They know the moment has passed, that they'll see each other again and will have nothing more to say. Haru drops Jacques off at his hotel and goes back to the house by the Kamo-gawa, then calls Manabu Umebayashi, a Japanese friend living in Paris, where he is well-connected in cultural circles. He asks him for the address of a certain Maud Arden, and, the next day, he sends a letter that says, If the child is mine, I am here. A few weeks stretch away into the mist until, finally, Haru receives an answer: The child is yours. If you try to see either one of us, I'll kill myself. Forgive me.

After a long period of feeling frightened, dumbstruck, clinging to the same invisible thread that had driven him to write to Maud, Haru did the one thing on earth he knew best: he got organized. To this end, after briefly prevaricating, he let the other resident master of organization in on the secret. Sayoko had opened the door to the messenger from destiny; she would be its sole witness, and he informed her that he would soon be the father of a French child whom he would not be allowed to see. "Not for the time being, in any case," he added, then said, "I'm telling you because there will be photographs." She nodded, went to the low table by the tree, and spent the next hour doing her bookkeeping. Finally, she got up and made Haru a cup of tea. "Will it be a girl?" she asked. He nodded, and she went away again.

Six months earlier, aspiring housekeepers had paraded through the room with the maple tree, but only Sayoko had stood out against the backdrop of the tree, with all the sharpness of a singular bough. Haru looked at her looking at the glass cage, and the pilgrim saw in her all the signs. Her home was where she had her husband and son, but the place where she had lived and would live her real life was the house by the Kamo-gawa. As it happened, she had all the skills required for the job, those that arrange what is visible, and those that subjugate what is invisible. What was more, she adored Keisuke, who was part of the furniture when he was sleeping off his sake on the sofa in the main room. According to her heterodox classification of Shinto and Buddhist deities, she was convinced he was a sort of hero, venerated by both religions, a belief she stood by despite his ferrety breath and excruciating snoring: since Keisuke saw things other people did not see, he had every reason to drink, so as to make his way through everyday life. Similarly, he needed a sanctuary where he could indulge his art and his grief, and that sanctuary was the house by the river looking out at the mountains. Sayoko, with her kimonos, her placid manner, and her genial talent for household management, knew this instinctively, and that was why she loved Haru but revered Keisuke.

In the weeks that followed, Haru arranged the new dance of his life. He wrote back to Maud: I will respect your wish; I will not try to see my daughter. Don't hurt yourself. Through the intermediary of Manabu Umebayashi, he hired a detective who spoke English and a photographer, gave them precise instructions, and paid them generously. In his study, he installed panels of cypress wood, then waited for the third thread of his narrative to come into the world. He placed Melland's gift on his desk: it was the cast of a little ivory-colored primitive statuette, which, he learned, represented a fertility goddess— destiny indeed, he mused. The summer was even warmer than usual, and he liked feeling the humid heat. Meanwhile, thanks to some unfathomable mechanism, his disdain for paternity was transformed into hope. Something inside him wanted that child born of the disaster, and an exquisite certainty even rooted itself inside him: she would come to his hillside one day and would, in turn, discover her own pilgrimage.

Amid the lingering summer days devoted to waiting, women, sake, and art, a particularly mild autumn arrived. On the mountains, the trees flowed like fire. In the far heavens, sprays of purple blooms were withering. The heart of ancient Japan beat in the red glow of the maple trees. As the days drew nearer to the birth of that foreign child, Haru felt a renewed love for his native land blossom inside him. On October 20, he was at home with Keisuke, sipping sake.

"I love Japan more and more," he declared, and Keisuke burst out laughing.

"You're a stranger here," he said, "that's why you sleep with Western women."

"I'm as Japanese as you are," Haru retorted, surprised.

Keisuke didn't say anything.

"I belong in Shinnyo-dō," Haru said, protesting further.

"You're a pilgrim," said the potter, "wandering through your own life. You may have found your house, but, deep down, you're a child of the mountains who has torn out his heart and gone into exile. And so to avoid rules, you avoid the truth."

"The truth?"

Keisuke chuckled.

"The truth: love."

Haru was about to answer, but the telephone rang, and he went to take the call from the new messenger of destiny. When he came back, Keisuke recited two lines from Rilke's poem to him, the next two from the same poem Haru himself had quoted to Melland:

"'And in the nights the heavy earth falls / From among the stars toward solitude.' Even Rilke understands your country better than you do."

But Haru didn't care. He didn't care about the earth of Japan, about exile and stars and solitude. He didn't care about all those things that, until now, had meant something to him. He waited for Keisuke to leave, and when Sayoko came to remove the sake service, he said, "Her name is Rose."

He pronounced it in the English manner, the language he was teaching Sayoko for when he hosted Western guests.

"Rose?" she echoed, pronouncing it the Japanese way.

He nodded, and she said nothing else and went back to her quarters. Later on, he took a bath, read for a while, switched off the light, and fell asleep in an awareness of grace.

He woke up in the middle of the night, and with the same certainty that had shown him the clouds gathered above his valley, he took fright at the thought of the future—of solitude, and the heavy earth—and for no reason he thought again of the fox and the reclusive lady, and he stood up and went to the maple in its cage. The tree was murmuring faintly, and, after a moment of distress, he understood its message. As usual, he could not hear the stars. As she had done every time, Maud had blinded him. She cast a harsh light on things, a light which, paradoxically, prevented him from seeing, and so he had been deluding himself, telling himself an absurd story in which he had control over things, imagining a future that had no possible existence. And yet, in the end, everything was transparent. His daughter was born now, and he would not know her. She had come from among the stars and was condemning him to solitude.

A nd so, because he could not change destiny, Haru Ueno changed himself, and from that night on, a series of transformations was born.

For a start, he learned. He found out where and with whom Maud lived; he retraced her history, her social cartography, her constellations of friends. In the space of a few weeks, he compiled a good amount of information about her. But he wasn't learning just for the sake of it. He learned to bring his desire to meet his daughter into the light. That desire couldn't stay buried. It weighed on him from the moment he woke up until late in the evening. It was changing his complicity with life. It separated him from the world with an invisible screen. Haru looked out at his mountains and felt nothing, only the memory of a vanished rapture. He navigated between a blind spot inside him and a faraway territory where the key to his identity was kept. Bit by bit, the certainty of self-knowledge he used to have was being eroded. Worse still, the only time he felt reborn—during his loop around Shinnyo-dō—gave way, at home by the Kamo-gawa, to even greater solitude.

Before long, he had so much information he didn't know what to do with it, like a snake that needs to digest, then fast, then shed its skin. He ruminated over this meal he'd been served, reading and rereading the reports, studying the photographs, feeling tormented by the sensation that he was *looking* at them but not *seeing*. There were the things they said, and the things they didn't say. They said: Maud Arden, twenty-eight years old, unmarried, dividing her time between Paris, where she worked, and the Vienne valley in Touraine, where her widowed mother, Paule Arden, lived. On one of the pictures, taken with a telephoto lens, he could see the layout of the property. Built on a height, it overlooked the river and faced rolling hills on the opposite shore. In the center of the garden stood a large house, harmoniously proportioned, with a wrought iron sun room and high windows. Haru thought the pale color of the stone was beautiful, as was the view over the valley, where the unfathomable was winding its way; equally lovely were the majestic trees on the estate. One day when no one was there, the photographer had gone inside the property and taken a great number of pictures. In the vast garden, which had no watercourses of any kind, the melody of a stream seemed to flow everywhere, and for that reason Haru thought he might look on Paule as an ally. She seemed to take long strides, then pause and look pensively up at the clouds, and in her movements, as caught by the camera, there was a fluidity in which he recognized the moving presence of the spirit. Tall and straight, with dark hair, she seemed to be the antithesis of her property, with its interlacing of climbing plants and old roses, a space in which one could immerse oneself as if in a secret pond. However incomprehensible her world appeared to him, Haru liked to think that in her garden she became liquid, that she loved the rain and would like the moss in Kyōto, and he supposed—or wanted to believe—that Rose owed her floral first name to her grandmother. Naturally, in the beginning, this breaking and entering into a stranger's life seemed reprehensible to him, as did his eagerness to receive the reports, or the long hours he spent going through them. In his study, all around him, a strange calm had gathered, the very substance of the air changed: his gaze shot through space, ten thousand kilometers away, to unveil another life—a life that was vastly different. Bit by bit, however, as he became enamored of that elegant woman, he felt less guilty. Every day, he addressed a silent prayer to her, expressing all his respect, but also all his gratitude.

Because his daughter was growing up with Paule. Haru came to know Rose in a Moses basket in the garden, in a baby carriage, and, with the arrival of spring, in the little playpen on the grass where he could truly see her for the first time: tiny, pale, with her red hair, while the tall dark-haired woman smiled as she leaned over her. Paule Arden had lost her husband very early in her marriage, but she was wealthy by birth and hadn't needed to work or remarry. She had a few friends in the neighboring town, picked her roses in the friendship of wind and rain and memories, and spent the better part of her days out-of-doors. Haru could think of no better tutor for his daughter than this dreaming star, accustomed to sadness and flowers. He looked at them laughing together and thought, This bond cannot be broken. About Maud's father, on the other hand, he had found out very little. It would seem that he had died an early death without leaving any trace in the world that was visible to the living, and if there were portraits and relics of him inside the house, Haru had no access to them. For a mysterious reason, he could sense that his daughter's fate was in the hands of women, without considering the fact that this intuition excluded him, as well: she was growing up without a father, as her mother had done before her; he was, in like fashion, a ghost whose portrait was nowhere to be seen. And besides, why should he think he was failing as a father when he knew that he was absolutely alive and present?

First, he digested this meal of information, examining the photographs of Rose, red-haired and laughing, adorable, lying in the grass, her forehead offered to the heavens. He never grew tired of gazing at her, and since then he felt he had the strength to fast, he granted himself a year of patience. He was no longer in any doubt that he would achieve his aims, and he went on living his life the way secret lovers do, with the prospect of a clandestine reunion, someday. Sayoko would come into the study, put down the tea or the sake, walk past the prints pinned on the cypress-wood panels, and go out again without saying a word. When Keisuke came over, Haru received him in the maple room, well away from his study, which had become a sanctuary connecting Kyōto to a cluster of faraway hills. He read stacks of books about France, carefully compiling a store of knowledge, but he didn't want to learn French: he would speak Japanese with his daughter, naturally. Finally, he wondered at length how to go about approaching Maud, and he decided he would write to Paule when Rose reached her first birthday.

But he did not write. There was what the reports said and what they didn't say. And what they didn't say, Haru could see. Maud went by train to her mother's place every weekend, and a few photographs showed her in the garden, smoking a cigarette, her back turned to the little playpen on the grass. On the morning of Rose's first birthday, Haru was reading in his study when Sayoko came in with the quarterly envelope from France. It contained photographs of a moving van outside the building in Paris where Maud lived, then outside Paule's house, with a short caption: She's moving house.

Haru raised his eyes toward his mountains. On the snapshots, the skies of Touraine were immense, curved into a vast lid over the green earth. He thought that, in Kyōto, there was no such vault, no infinity, only the mists rising along the slopes in the evening. The leaves of the cherry and maple trees on the banks of the Kamo-gawa were beginning to turn red, the morning joggers trotted by in silence, space and time came undone, Haru's life split apart. One photograph showed Maud, arms crossed, in front of the sun room, but in actual fact it showed no one. A childhood memory came to him, of a Noh play at the nearby shrine, haunted by spectral forms and lost women, against a backdrop of screens and mountain pines. He remembered it as if from a dream, something no subsequent theater performance had been able to erase, a shadowy dream that stayed inside him and permeated his years. Maud was moving into her mother's place as if she were taking the veil, withdrawing from the world, with the gaze of a ghost, and he did not doubt that she would kill herself if he reentered her life. The irony of fate: his business had never been better, and he was devastated by the thought that his success was growing in proportion to his heart's distress, that he was only a well-known art dealer because he had failed to become a father. Until now his life had contained only promises of conquest, and now it could be seen from a different angle: it had been ripped apart like a piece of tissue paper, and someone—that woman—had kept the scattered shreds. Tragedy no longer belonged to the outside world: it had crept inside him, and he was sentenced to continue fasting. And so, since he did not want to accept this equation of fate, but could not solve it from without, he shed his skin.

H e shed his skin with the determination he applied to everything, and to do this, he returned to the heart he'd once torn from the mountains, looking not to the future but to the past. He went to Takayama.

In the town, he visited his father and brother and found the former tired, the latter worried. They drank sake and exchanged news, briefly. As Haru was taking his leave, Naoya followed him outside, and, his back to the shop, he said, "His mind is going, you know." Haru walked back up the street of sake shops, an opening of space-time which led to the shades of old Japan. He thought, Kyōto is its lungs, Takayama its heart, a simple, fervent heart, rooted in these ageless houses adrift on the surf of time. He took the road toward the family house, a fifteen-minute drive from the center of town. In his youth, his father used to walk down from the mountain every morning. Sometimes he'd stay to sleep in town, above the shop. Otherwise he would walk in the moonlight on a frozen night, following the torrent to the house at its edge. In the middle of the ford, there was a huge boulder, and in winter only its frozen cap showed above the water. Haru had grown up watching the snow fall and melt on that rock, had taken from it his love for matter and his intelligence regarding form. He often thought he'd received less from his father than from his stream or, rather, that what he'd learned from his family—unbeknownst to them—was what he didn't want. Toil, eat, sleep, and start again. Labor did not give way to contemplation but to the absence of labor. There was time only for a rough material in which no one could see the hidden form. But the watercourse outside the house said, The world asks for nothing more than to express form. Work hard to open invisible doors.

In proportion to the distancing from his foreign child, Haru searched for new roots in his own culture. The largest of the invisible doors, the one that would lead to the others, went by the name of tea. Haru was willing to walk without stopping, provided the paving stones were bathed in pure water. Life must be a path washed by gentle rain, under a sky of ever-changing transparency. In the cool air, in the shifting light, lay the rolling hills of a land where you could worship beauty and believe in the spirit. And in Takayama he knew where and with whom he could go through that door. He drove along the stream, headed down a track through the trees, and parked on the shoulder before continuing on foot. He could hear the torrent and the murmur of the wind in the pine trees; rays of sunlight angled through the branches with a quiver of stained glass. The cabin came into view, the thatched roof, the wooden veranda, the vegetable garden at the edge of the stream, and, floating over it all, an atmosphere of solitude and strength. It was November, and on the far bank, the leaves of a young maple tree were taking flight, russet and frail, new and already dying. There was no one. Haru went to the stream, sat on the veranda overlooking the marrow plants and the shiso leaves, and let himself go to the rush of the rapids. A noise roused him from his daydreaming, and Jirō, emerging from the woods, came to join him under the roof of the veranda, then motioned to him to come in. The old man had an antique store in town, where squalor and treasures lived side-by-side. On the mountain, he reigned over a kingdom of austerity and grace. In the main room, he invited his guest to sit down while he went to prepare the tea. In Kyōto,

Haru had taken part in many tea ceremonies and known many moments of ecstasy and disappointment. Sometimes the magic was there; other times, in a cold and formal atmosphere, he had to maintain a pose of polite boredom. But it was always a celebration of the civilization of tea. One bathed in the same river where masters of old had been, one understood the lesson of elegant sobriety and refined humility. Jirō, on the other hand, officiated amid the chaos of a cabin strewn with books, things, and various implements. There were no scrolls on the walls or flowers in the alcove. In the entrance were stacks of beer crates. The tatami were old and slightly shabby. To one side, through the sliding door, a cluttered kitchen was visible. It was a clean place, but everything was topsy turvy.

And yet, spirit spoke to spirit there. A cast iron kettle, set on an enameled stand, hummed above a little charcoal fire. Around Jirō, the tea instruments were laid out in no particular order, along with a pitcher of fresh water. Sitting cross-legged, he began whipping the green powder, laughing all the while. One day he had said to Haru, "What more do you need, besides some mountain water and a little bit of fantasy? I don't understand those expensive tea ceremonies they perform with their glum faces." In fact, although Jirō did not observe many of the ceremony's codes and rituals, in his home the way of tea sparkled. It sparkled in the impeccable cleanliness of the utensils, the purity of the water, the shimmering shadows of the trees. It sparkled in the intention and modesty of the setting, in the precise gestures of a warm-hearted man. It was a dull sparkle, without brilliance, a sparkle of camaraderie—the workings of tea came alive and drew you to them through the bonds of friendship. The outside world shivered, the room became a presence, the here and now glittered, and, for an hour, two friends lived side-by-side outside time.

Haru drank the first thick tea, a bitter paste that tasted of vegetables and forest.

"What are you doing in town?" asked the old man.

"I came to see my father."

"Oh," said Jirō, "surely not."

He reached for Haru's bowl, refilled it with water, whipped the residue of the paste from its sides into a froth.

"How is your business doing?" he asked.

"It's doing very well."

Jirō placed the bowl in front of him on the tatami.

"Shamefully well, even," Haru added.

The old man laughed.

"We're in trade," he said. "Shame is our daily bread."

"I'm not ashamed of making money," said Haru.

"I mean the shame of having to please," said Jirō.

Haru took a sip of the second, lighter tea.

"I don't try to please," he said.

"You do it instinctively, but you do," said Jirō, "and it's still vulgar."

In the distance, a raven cawed, and it occurred briefly to Haru that the torrent split life in two. The sun filtered through the leaves and showed him the opposing riverbanks of his life. On one, there were women, sake, business dinners, and parties. On the other, there were works of art, Keisuke, and Tomoo. In the center, in a zone of mystery washed with flowing water, floated Rose, enigmatic and ethereal.

"Tell yourself any story you like," said Jirō. "In the end, you'll be alone with your stories, and you'll see whether they console you or fill you with pain."

"I think I know who I am," said Haru.

"Then what are you doing here?"

Haru was about to reply, I'm visiting an old master, but a faint breeze set the *fūrin* bell at the entrance to chiming. Outside, the stream was rushing, the wind was humming through the trees, and through the tea he was wandering in the sweet madness of things. A strange sensation spread slowly through his chest.

Could Jirō be right? he wondered. And, for the first time in his life: Could I be kidding myself? Jirō had leaned back against the wall, his eyes closed. What do we go looking for in tea if not the invisible? Haru thought. Again it occurred to him that that woman had taken something from him, or, perhaps, she had marked out a territory inside him where he was walking blind. The two friends sat on in silence, and Haru acknowledged the coolness bathing his spirit now. Although it was shot through with rustling sounds and faraway calls, it was the coolness of the void which the way of tea offered its pilgrims. Life was being stripped of its ornaments, and, as at Shinnyo-dō, was offering itself to him without finery. He was strolling through a valley where stars dwelt, and he hoped that this time he would know how to listen to them. Are they bringing the words of my ancestors? Of my brothers? Of my judges? he wondered. And, troubled by this unusual trilogy, he sensed an intuition was forming.

Jirō opened his eyes.

"A man who thinks he knows himself is dangerous," he said.

Haru stood up.

"By the way," the old man added, "your father isn't doing well."

When Haru didn't reply, he added, "Don't you want the truth? You will know desolation."

Armed with Jirō's admonition, determined to listen to the stars, Haru began by taking his ancestors' lead: he went looking for the truth from his father. And found his mother there.

Or rather, he found silence and solitude, and sitting between them, a woman, bent over the kitchen table, slicing matsutake. In the nascent twilight, he could smell their fragrance. He turned on the light switch, and she raised her surprised eyes to him, then came to greet him, joyfully, accompanied by the silence and solitude, which seemed to move with her. Fleetingly, he sensed he was in a familiar room where an identical scene would play over and over—she would be waiting in the darkness, look up at him with surprise, come to him with joy—but already she was making him sit down, pouring him tea, asking him questions about his health, his business, his life in Kyōto. When she fell silent, he pointed at the mushrooms.

"Naoya picked them this morning," she said.

"They cost a fortune at the market," he said.

She laughed.

"Even the poor are rich."

With an indecipherable expression on her face, she added, "I'm making them for dinner. Your father and brother will be home soon."

"Naoya is having dinner here?" he asked, astonished.

She nodded, said nothing more. She put some rice in a

cast iron pot, along with some sake, mirin, soy sauce, dashi, and the mushrooms, sprinkled with salt. She mixed it all, then covered the pot with a white kitchen towel, her movements precise, wrapped in silence. He turned his head, and through the window in the fading daylight, he saw the dark pine trees against a background of diluted ink. The torrent was rushing down the slope of his childhood, taking with it his ancestors' voices, arousing conflicting desires in him for intimacy and flight. While he drifted through this ballet of shadows, his father and brother appeared and, in their wake, the odor of yeast from the brewery, the one he'd known all through childhood. They washed their hands, and Haru thought it took his father an unusually long time. Now his mother had placed the pot on the flame to simmer, and as she served the sake, layers of time came loose. Every action and every word seemed isolated from the others, coated with sadness. The disjointed conversation, his father's figure at the sink, and the cold bite of the alcohol failed to connect.

"Why do you always come in spring?" his father asked suddenly.

"I come every season," Haru replied, surprised.

"And yet the best season is autumn," his father went on, not hearing him.

Haru wanted to say something, but Naoya motioned to him discreetly.

"Yes, autumn," his father insisted, "most good things happen in autumn."

His mother's face had set into an unfamiliar mask, and Haru thought again of the Noh play he'd seen as a child, of its terrifying ghosts, its décor of mountains and fear. Is this the lesson of my ancestors? he wondered. A father who is still young but already losing his mind? His mother laid the table, brought the rice with mushrooms and served them, unusually slowly. Outside, darkness was falling, and at the same time, a sort of lightweight crepe cloth fell unexpectedly over Haru's perception. They ate their meal in a deep, irrevocable, eternal night. From time to time, Haru's father nodded and murmured something to himself, and Haru was overcome by dark shadows. He thought he ought to tear himself away from this scene peopled with ghosts, but just then his mother smiled at him, and he remembered one of Keisuke's stories. Just before the end of the Heian period, a monk informs his mother that he dreams of making a pilgrimage to China. The journey to the Mountain of the Five Terraces, a sacred Buddhist site, will take three years. The mother is eighty years old. These are the last convulsions of the era, and she knows she won't be there for the next one. And yet, her shocked silence lingers, and the son leaves the room. A few months go by, suspended in time, filled with worry, until one morning, he informs her that he will be leaving soon. Once again, sorrow prevents the old woman from speaking; once again, the son leaves the room, and, while she is waiting for the hour of their farewell, he goes away without coming back to see her. She doesn't blame him: she reproaches herself for her silence, weeps so hard she cannot breathe, and writes the journal of her suffering, mingled with superb poems. At the end of all this, she wants to die. "I don't see the point," Haru had said, at that stage in the story. "Don't you see the grandeur in loving an ungrateful person?" Keisuke asked.

Haru took a sip of sake and looked at his father. Do I have taste because my heart is incompetent? he wondered, troubled by the thought that art was perhaps the fleshless part of love—the part without ghosts, without distress. An insidious, unpleasant thought was working its way through him. Didn't this absence of flesh imply the shriveling of his soul? Had he spent his whole life running away from sharing any closeness with his loved ones, with their suffering and their fate? And then the veil that had been distorting his perception vanished, and he saw the scene differently. The shadows had given way to a glow, where gestures and gazes melded together in the same warm space. The room smelled of humus, of rain and cold earth, and in this fragrance of undergrowth, a family was having dinner. Haru asked his brother a few questions about the brewery, and Naoya, initially reticent, answered with increasing good grace. Their father joined in the conversation without a sour note, and they sipped their after-dinner sake, casually conversing. At one point Haru told the story of how they'd transported a dead-drunk Keisuke in a wheelbarrow from a neighboring construction site, and there were peals of laughter. The world had split in two again—outside, the protective immensity of the mountains and trees; inside, the gentle, sad, deep, and inaccessible protection his family gave him. Finally, *elsewhere*, motionless and secret, the stars kept watch.

Haru went back to his car after saying goodbye to his parents and his brother where they stood together in the little entrance. In the rearview mirror, he intuited, more than he actually saw, his mother waving her hand, and he raised his own in return. He was twenty minutes from the inn, twenty minutes which, he sensed, would determine his destiny as a father—twenty minutes, he thought, and all the strength of the sake and tea. He drove past the little shrine where he'd seen the Noh play, but he no longer feared his spectral memories. His father's figure was with him, his solitude and distress banished by the presence of kindly ancestors. He saw him again, from the time of his childhood, in the back room at the brewery, drinking and chatting with his neighbors in trade. Around him a cloth of silk unfurled, and Haru could see the threads being woven and unwoven as the years went by. But the weft of it always found its shape again, and it was the birth of his sons, the affection of the local people, the force of the torrent, the joy of the mountain—yes, it was all of that, and far more besides, on the map of a territory where people and places respected one another. Haru turned the car around and drove back to the shrine, got out, and, walking through the orange torii, went up the path to the altar. There was a smell of resin and bark in the air. He stood motionless, vigilant, as if sharpened, sensing a presence, and before long, as he combed through the darkness, he thought he could see his mother approaching, taking small, deferential steps. He recalled how she would hold his hand, teaching him to appease the *kami* of rice and sake, laughing if he missed when he tossed the coin. He turned and started back to the torii, went through it, bowed, then headed again toward the altar. He tossed a coin into the offering box and rang the bell: the night welcomed him. He clapped his hands twice and waited: the world was vibrating. Somewhere, Keisuke's voice resonated, saying: humans, humans, humans. Of course, thought Haru, there are only humans, but I must go to the shrine to be able to hear them and see them. He recalled his father, at the dinner table, murmuring to himself. He thought, suddenly, My daughter was born in the autumn, the season of good things!

When he was back on the road to the inn, with the pine trees rushing past him, thrust like spears toward the indulgence of the clouds, he was embraced by tenderness and solitude. No matter which period of his childhood he recalled, it was bathed in sweetness but devoid of closeness—is that why I left? he wondered. Now he saw the next stage of his life begin to take shape before him. His daughter was the flesh of his love for art, its true incarnation and essential purpose, the redemption of his early disappointment and betrayal. With her autumnal radiance, she brought light to his hibernal heart, and if he was bound to cherish her in silence, he could endure it—even the poor are rich, he said out loud, and laughed.

He came to Kakurezato—he'd let them know he'd be late—at around midnight. They gave him a warm welcome and invited him to sit by the still-warm fireplace in the middle of the large foyer, and they brought him a hot towel, some sake, and an autumn manjū. The dirt floor, the high wooden roof structure, the paper partitions at the windows, the calligraphy, and the pottery in the alcove: it was all just as he remembered from long ago. He spoke for a moment with Tomoko, the innkeepers' daughter, who'd been at school with him. She asked him about his work and gave him news of their mutual acquaintances. Behind her, above a bouquet of maple branches, hung the ink drawing of a closed circle. Haru preferred open *enso*, but this evening, that closed loop was pleasing to him: he wondered what he would tell Rose about it, and he was so moved that he stopped listening to the young woman. The future was full of light. The scene inhabited by ghosts was replaced by a conversation of the living; he could not see his daughter, but he could speak to her, and because he was a servant of the spirit, he thought, The spirit will carry my words to her. He stared at the *enso* on its square of matte paper and realized that Tomoko had fallen silent.

"Forgive me," he said, "I'm tired."

She smiled.

"Nothing changes here," she said. "But your life in Kyōto must be fascinating."

And as he was nodding absentmindedly, she added, "Your father is not well, you know."

He lowered his gaze, embarrassed.

"He's young," Tomoko said. "The sorrow will last a long time."

"He doesn't seem unhappy," said Haru.

"The sorrow is yours," she said gently. "Sorrow is for those who love their absent ones."

He took a sip of sake.

"I know," he said, "I know it only too well."

She laughed, in a kindly way.

"A woman?" she asked.

It was his turn to laugh. She smiled and stood up.

"We've left the bath open for you," she said. "Now it's time for you to get some rest."

He thanked her and headed toward his room. There, he put on the yukata provided by the inn before going back out into the gloom of the corridor to make his way to the hot springs. The roof structure of the old building, brown in color and prominent, ran like a spider's web above the passage. In the beams, something was murmuring, and as he entered the steaming water, he could hear the sound even more intensely. Despite the darkness, the vast room was still a place of light: the wood glossed with moonlight, the water lacquered with clarity. The big hinoki-wood bath, polished with use, was next to a glass pane which had no visible window frame and was stretched like a canvas over the landscape of waterfalls. In the foreground, he could make out the trunks of cypress trees, and at their foot, enkianthus shrubs whose red foliage, in the dark, was gilded with mercury. Haru knew that it was all beautiful, but he felt nothing. He was absorbed by the sound growing ever louder, which came neither from the torrent nor from the inn, something he'd never heard that was still, somehow, familiar.

He floated in the water without moving, abandoned himself to the flow and the stones, to the stars and trees, to Japan and the sleeping mountains. A long moment passed, then a cloud veiled the moon. There was a sudden shower, and the waters of the bath, the rapids, and the sky were mingled.

He entered the night. Entered with gratitude, moved toward the invisible, bowed more deeply than he'd ever bowed. Through the ferns on the riverbanks, on the stage of a moonlit shadow play, the web of his life became visible. He heard his mother's voice saying, Your ablutions are like a raven's, and the cawing of the ravens in Kyōto blended with fragmented memories of the past. He saw himself with her at the *sentō*, she was helping him wash at the taps along the wall across from the basin. Only ravens wash quickly, she said, and he remembered, too, that in the evening she told him the legend of the hamlet hidden at the bottom of the stream that had given its name to the inn: it only surfaced for humans to see on the night of the solstice, before returning at dawn to its shroud of eddies and rock. That is the canvas of my life, thought Haru, but my hours of deepest perception usually come in November and May. The night expanded and, with it, his mother's lesson, the wisdom of long ablutions, the slowness of steps. The night said, You are a child of the mountain, a native of Shinnyo-dō, a passenger of strangeness, a solitary pilgrim. The night said: Give honor. A heavy rain transformed the massif of pine trees on the riverbank into a cloud from the depths of the heavens. A leaf fell past the window, and Haru thought: the sky is withering. The rain stopped, and the stars came out.

And then he saw the fox. It seemed to be walking on water, crossing the current. At the middle of the ford it paused, turned toward him, then, continuing on its way, it reached the opposite bank and disappeared into the cover of pine trees. The night-time murmuring he'd heard earlier grew more intense now. Haru slipped deeper into the bath, let the water cover his face. He meditated for a long time and did not go back to his room until dawn. His futon had been prepared, and, in keeping with the tradition of the inn, a poem had been left there. Haru sat facing the large, frameless windowpane, which was set straight into the wall and overlooked the torrent. His father and mother and brother, and everyone from this place, stood there, imperceptible yet palpable, in a row all together in front of the peaks, members of the mountain fraternity. Was the fox destined to show them to me? he wondered, and he saw Maud again in the bath as she had been on that first night. His memory restored her face to him with photographic precision, just as it had been as he finished the story about the lady and the fox from Heian. What did I say to her? he thought, stunned by the sadness he'd discovered in her, and what stunned him even more, How could I have failed to see it? There before him, the flow of the stream grew whiter, and its hidden hamlet, the outline of the cypress trees, all equally visible and invisible, brought an inaudible message. He lay down and read the poem aloud.

autumnal mountain—
so many stars
so many distant ancestors

A circle formed before his eyes, opening and closing in a continual fluid movement. In a perpetual autumn, mountains, stars, and unknown ancestors followed, preceded one another. He brought to mind his parents and brother sitting at the dinner table in the old house, wrapped in a glow of tenderness and fear. He saw himself as a child in the aisles at the brewery, giddy from the yeast, proud of his father's vigor, then as an indifferent young man eager to get away from this world of toil

and silence. I tore myself away from the mountains, he thought.
I wanted to flee the solitude, and I took it with me. Revisiting
the profile of his loved ones in the evening light, he thought,
I'm far away now, but this thread must not be broken. And so,
continuing the meditation he'd begun in the Takayama night,
he understood at last the murmuring he'd heard there.

After a sleepless night, he went to the common room, and there he found Akiyo, Tomoko's mother, who brought him tea and sat by the table to chat. She was wearing an autumn kimono embroidered with, among other flowers, camellias and campanulas in the shape of little stars. One of the breakfast dishes was rice with matsutake.

"I had some for dinner at my mother's, but you can never have enough," he said.

"Naoya sold them to us yesterday," she said with a laugh, "he's the best mushroom picker in the district."

They spoke about this and that, then he thanked her for the poem.

"It's by a contemporary poetess," she said. "I think she's still alive."

Seeing his surprise, she added, "You can be modern and deep at the same time."

"That's my job," he said.

She smiled and poured him some more tea.

"Just before dawn I saw a fox fording the torrent," he said.

"Fording it? Impossible, this time of year."

At the train station, he returned the car to an employee whose family he'd known since childhood. The man patted him affably on the shoulder. How could I have forgotten my people? he wondered. On the platform, a light snow had begun to fall. Haru let a snowflake land on his tongue, and it seemed to concentrate all the tastes of Takayama; he felt even greater regret at leaving his mountains. In the train, he slept intermittently. Words came back to him repeatedly, words he'd said in the bath at the time of Maud's sadness. In Kyōto, he took a cab to the house and found Sayoko sitting at her accounts book. She looked at him, not saying a thing, but from the way she pushed her glasses down her nose, he knew he ought to speak to her.

"It was snowing in Takayama," he said.

She gave him a stern look.

"We had matsutake to eat," he added.

Her gaze remained steady, and he relented: "My father is not doing well."

She narrowed her eyes.

"His mind?" she asked.

He nodded, used to her astonishing intuition. She made a gesture of compassion, placing her hand on her left collarbone.

"But Rose is well?" she asked.

Surprised, he nodded again; they had not spoken about Rose since the year of her birth. Sayoko went away, taking small, satisfied steps toward the kitchen, then she came back with the tea, sat down across from him, and went on with her bookkeeping. Finally, as he was getting ready to leave, she told him that Keisuke was at Tomoo's place.

To each other they said only the names of their dead: these were the words that, on that first evening, had filled Maud's eyes with sadness. As it happened, he'd heard these words from a brother, and it was his brothers who were waiting now on the path the stars revealed. In Takayama, he had drunk with his ancestors, in Kyōto, he would drink with Keisuke; as was fitting, Sayoko was showing him the way. He would go to Tomoo's place. He went on foot, crossing the Kamo-gawa, cutting through the university campus until he came to the shrine at Yoshida, where he climbed the wooded hillside of the same name. The weather was mild, and there was a hint of snow in the air. At the top of the hill, as he emerged from the cover of the trees, he came upon a raven and a priest he knew, having a conversation. The raven, a black form against an orange background, was perched on a torii. The priest, dressed in black, stood out against an immaculate white wall. Slightly higher up was a cluster of wooden buildings and altars, granite lanterns—the little fellow shrine of Takenaka, its tombs and stone foxes buried in the vegetation. From there, the way down the hill went along a lane surmounted by twenty or more torii interwoven with tall cherry trees; from there, too, one had the finest view onto the neighboring hill of Shinnyo-dō and the mountains of the East. The gong of the Hōnen-in sounded in the distance, and transfigured time became presence. The place was now one of breath and peace, sighs were everywhere in the tall trees, the cries of birds turned into whispers. This priest was famously not in his right mind; he spoke to living ravens and stone foxes in a language only they could understand, but which he nevertheless used in the presence of his flock. He was popular, regardless, and no one would ever dream of abandoning him. Haru walked past and greeted him. The priest, deep in conversation, bowed and gave him a smile, and only when Haru was already some way past did he call out to him.

"What's that noise you're dragging along behind you?" he said.

"What noise?" asked Haru.

The raven let out a squawk.

"I don't know," answered the priest, "but we can hear it."

They chatted about this and that, but before long Haru felt he heard the words and sounds of the world as if they were being made *elsewhere*. He was alone in an unfamiliar territory that was being swept along by its own murmuring, and it was

only outside him that the flow of real things was happening.
He lost the thread of the old priest's chatter, looked up at the
lowering sky—a sky of snow, he thought, but I'm not alone.
And so he laughed, and, interrupting the man of the cloth, he
said, "You want to know what that noise is? It's my ancestors."

"Ah!" said the priest. "I knew it!"

And, turning to the raven: "It's his ancestors."

After which, he obligingly translated this into the raven's
language. Haru looked at the entrance to Takenaka, framed
by two white stone sculptures of foxes, and, stunned to find
himself at the entrance to a shrine devoted to Inari, a goddess
in the shape of a fox, he said to the priest, "In Takayama I saw
a fox walking on water."

"In Takayama?" said the priest.

"Kakurezato, to be exact."

"Kakurezato?" he mumbled. "I don't understand a thing
about those legends of hidden hamlets."

"But the fox wasn't hidden," said Haru.

"Of course not," answered the priest. "What's invisible is
never hidden."

Haru bade him farewell, went back down the hill of Yoshida,
and started up that of Shinnyo-dō. Just as he reached the temple,
small, placid snowflakes began to fall. The stone lanterns shone
in the fading daylight; beyond the rooftops, the mountains kept
watch, and Haru silently recited the lines of the living poetess.
He thought about his daughter and saw her bathed in the colors
of that moment. Inari orange and fox fur were reflected in the
russet of her hair. Leaning over her in the black sky were the
dead of Heian, the mountain ancestors, the white stars in the
autumn night. As he walked around the temple and under a
vault of flamboyant maple trees, he once again recalled Maud's
face in the bath that first night. My ancestors are alive, but hers
are dead, he thought. I did not know that the deceased, too,

could be dead or alive. He walked on a little further and stopped at the top of the steps that led down to his friend's house, where the notes of a piano and joyful voices could be heard. Sakura, Tomoo's little dog, was yapping, then came several bars of jazz and sudden peals of laughter.

He realized that these solitary moments on the threshold of the loving home were a foreshadowing of his life to come. From that night on, he would be situated between two worlds, between the dead and the living, between darkness and the bright light of dwellings, between the past and the future, and in that place, he would speak to his daughter. The dead had the power to give joy or despair, he thought, and he had to make it possible for Rose to hear the voice of her mountain ancestors. Then another thought came to replace that one, and, stunned and moved, he said to himself, It's thanks to her that I can hear that voice. At the same time, inside the house, Keisuke shouted, More sake! and Haru came down the steps, savoring his last breath of bittersweet solitude. The evening was beginning, ushered in by its invisible powers; the day was dying, burying its hidden sorrows. Haru held his daughter close in his thoughts, the way he would have held her in his arms, and he went to join his community of brothers.

And these brothers, it must be said, were not very presentable. What Haru could tell from the scene before him was that they'd been drinking and singing and asking for more sake, and when they finished, they'd started all over again. At this point they were eating a little something, careful never to forget to drink. At the piano, a young musician was playing "Bemsha Swing." Above the keyboard were photographs of Tomoo's three idols: Kazuo Ōno, Thelonius Monk, and Federico Fellini. Sprawled next to Tomoo was the handsome Isao, his only love. All around, a cluster of the faithful of both sexes were munching and drinking as they chatted.

Haru was greeted with a joyful clamor, and they poured him a drink. Keisuke shot him a mocking look, Sakura came to lick his hand, and the party continued on its merry way. First there was jazz, then Tomoo and Isao, in top form, put on a parody of a Noh play. They wore themselves out shouting at the top of their lungs, exaggerating their movements. There was a great deal of laughter, and more conversation, and once night had fallen a young woman sang old Amami songs. Through the window they could see the snowflakes drifting lazily past the streetlamp, which had come on at five o'clock, and everyone looked and listened, leaning against the walls. Beyond them, the light carved out the branches of a Japanese cherry tree; the young woman sang "in search of new lands," and the guests' expressions turned serious. Despite our wanderings, we take serious things seriously, thought Haru, and he was relieved of a burden, the nature of which he failed to understand. "By one hundred carpenters," the song continued, and he could feel the wooden house all around him, so similar to a huge sailing ship. Finally they applauded the singer, and Haru went to sit next to Keisuke. He told him the story of his stay in Takayama, spoke about his father, the matsutake, Jirō, Kakurezato, and the fox crossing the torrent on a phantom ford. Finally, he reported in detail his conversation with the priest at Yoshida, and Keisuke, who'd been listening in silence—but drinking all the while—burst out laughing at his final words.

"Sometimes, priests do make sense!"

"I can't stop hearing his words in my mind," said Haru. "What is not hidden that I should be seeing?"

"That's not what the good man was suggesting," said Keisuke.

After looking at him thoughtfully, he added, "You're not telling me everything."

Just then, a young man stood up and left the room, while the guests encouraged him noisily.

"I listen to the stars," said Haru. "Maybe the fox was their messenger."

Keisuke burst out laughing again.

"What sort of gibberish is that?" he asked. "You can't even hear your own voice, so listening to the stars—I'd love to see that, never mind your idiotic Inari things."

Haru smiled.

"Humans, humans, humans," he said.

"Precisely," said Keisuke. "Only humans can deal with humans—I'm pretty sure that foxes and goddesses don't give a damn."

The young artist had come back into the room, wearing a long red wig that went all the way down to his ankles at the back, and to his hips in the front. He was standing motionless in the middle of the room, and everyone was singing his praises (and singing for more sake). "The lion! The lion!" shouted Isao. Tomoo went to fetch a little screen decorated with red peonies, set it up next to the actor, and the dance began. Haru, who was not crazy about kabuki, laughed heartily as the lion stamped his foot and swayed his hips, fired up by the peonies fluttering past his nostrils: this was one of the rare examples of the genre that Haru found entertaining. What made it even funnier was that Sakura was running in circles around the dancer, barking and growling at him, and at the end Keisuke whispered to Haru, "If he ever stops brawling in bars, he'll become a great actor." After that, the party continued with even more laughter and sake. Keisuke and Haru conversed, and outside, the snow was falling, hiding the stars, blanketing the city. For a while now, Haru had been feeling the way he had in Takayama, that a thin piece of crepe had been placed before his eyes. Puzzled, he thought, The murmurings have disappeared, but the veil is back, and he fell silent, letting the others chatter around him. The young pianist, completely drunk, was picking out the notes of "My One and Only Love," and Isao was serving rice with dried alevin to the guests. He handed a bowl to Tomoo and gave him an indefinable smile full of secret, intangible intimacy. Haru looked at the two men. Until then, Haru had only thought of Isao in terms of his youth and beauty, but tonight he simply saw him *there*, incarnate and present in the waltz of tenderness and invisible shared secrets—Everything is invisible, and everything is there in front of us, he thought, nothing is hidden, provided you try to see. Isao's pure profile, his slow gestures, his gray eyes did not speak of beauty, but of love, a love outside any norms or family, mysterious and whole. Keisuke said something to Haru that he didn't catch; he closed his eyes, thought of his daughter, understood that the veil was the sign of his indifference and surrender. And the ancestors' murmurings came back and, with them, the sharp image of Rose's face. He realized Keisuke was speaking to him, and he returned to the hubbub in the room, where the poet again said to him, "You're not telling me everything."

Haru didn't answer. He was meditating. All around him: snow, the dark sky, the stars. He was at home here. He had chosen these men and women, these artists and merchants, these joyful servants of the spirit. He looked carefully at every one of them, imagined introducing them to Rose, invented happy years where they would come to know each other. He laughed when Keisuke got unsteadily to his feet then tripped on the lion's wig and crashed onto the screen with the peonies. There were exclamations, there was applause, drowned out in no time by Keisuke's snoring. Haru raised his cup in Tomoo's direction, and Tomoo smiled at him. A sudden gust of wind sent the snowflakes into a whirl, and, enveloped by a sensation of emptiness mixed with warmth, Haru smiled back at Tomoo, smiled at his father, his mother, Naoya, the fox at the torrent, his ancestors, the stars, the ghosts of Shinnyo-dō, the spirits of Japan, and his carpenter brothers. Finally, while gazing at his friends gathered there, he smiled to his faraway daughter, who brought the divided souls together.

Homes like Haru's and Tomoo's that broke with tradition, compared to other Japanese households, by receiving guests round the clock, were also unusual for hosting as many women as they did men. There were no exclusively male parties, and women took part in the discussions and the festivities. Most of them were Japanese artists, but sometimes foreign artists or personalities were among these female guests. Press attachés would call Tomoo and say, Madam So-and-So from America or Germany will be giving a talk or a concert in Kyōto, and Tomoo would organize a reception in honor of Madam So-and-So from America or Germany. When a Madam So-and-So began coming regularly, he might occasionally even offer to have her stay, and despite the freezing cold room, with its Spartan futon, she wanted nothing more than to stay there, at Tomoo's. At dawn, Isao would bring her a strong coffee, then take her on a walk to the highest step on the Kurodani to watch the sun rise over the city. At her feet was the rustling of the old town of temples, on the horizon, the mountain crests, and all around them stirred the tombs of an unfamiliar civilization. Madam So-and-So fell—mentally—to her knees while, shivering, she took Isao's arm, then returned to the sailing ship, transported by unspeakable joy.

That very evening, a French pianist by the name of Emmanuelle Revers came to Shinnyo-dō. It was the third time she had visited Tomoo's home, but, for some reason or another, it was the first time Haru actually met her. He saw her enter the room, acknowledged her beauty, and sensed that she was a piece in the puzzle of his life. He thought she must be in her forties, but wasn't sure, as was often the case when he tried to guess a Western woman's age. Dark hair, dark skin, a slender body: she looked like a landscape that changed with the light, projecting bursts of shadow. Isao asked her if she was tired from the trip, if she wanted to retire to her room—she didn't, she was glad to have company: "I've been feeling rather lonely since I got here," she said. Tomoo led her over to Haru, the only one, other than himself, who spoke decent English. Her laughter was abrupt, her movements gentle, and her conversation pleasant and lively, as she was. At one point they joked about how cold it was in the house, and about Isao's icy early morning jaunts, and she said, "But I've never felt closer to the heart of my life."

She thought for a moment and corrected herself: "To the heart of life itself."

Later, she pointed to the photograph on the piano of Kazuo Ōno, the master of the *butō*.

"I saw him play in Tōkyō," she said. "I didn't understand a thing, but afterwards I wept for a long time. I was alone in my hotel room, and I lay sobbing in my bed and could not stop."

Tomoo smiled at her.

"The *butō* goes deep into our darkest places," he said.

She paused for a moment to consider his words.

"I see," she said eventually.

She stood up, went to the piano, reached for some sheet music and began to play. Haru came to sit close by, admiring her fine profile, without desiring her, glad simply that she was there, and he began to feel something that gave substance to what he'd perceived at the beginning, and which the conversation had subsequently hidden: there was a sadness about her, now revealed by her playing. They chatted intermittently between pieces of music, and much later he glanced at his watch and saw that it was three o'clock in the morning. In the middle of the room, lying on his screen, Keisuke gave a grunt. Emmanuelle laughed.

"Last time, he was more talkative," she said.

"Keisuke is a great storyteller," said Haru, "I think he tells stories even in his dreams."

"Would you like to take a short walk in the snow before you go?" she asked suddenly.

She was looking at him sweetly.

"With pleasure," he said, "but aren't you tired?"

"I am tired," she said, "but I haven't been out of doors since I got to Japan."

They put their coats on and went out. It had stopped snowing. They went up the steps, through the maple trees, around the back of the temple, and found themselves alone in the silent courtyard. The sky was clearing; beneath the restored presence of the stars, the mild, humid air was turning cold, and a layer of snow covered the paths. The top of the great pagoda stood out in the dark as patches of white roof, the stone lanterns flickered, the tree branches made sketches of ink and chalk on the night. While they were talking, Haru noticed a strange cracking inside him—the cracking of an ice floe, he thought, and, disconcerted by the image, he suggested they continue on to Kurodani.

"I'm spoiling Isao's hospitality, but this first snow has invited us," he said.

They wove their way through the cemeteries and reached the top of the great steps. Below them was the faint hum of the sleeping city. On the slope of the hill, the ravens' tombs and trees stood in a row, dusted with freshly fallen snow. Blurred by darkness, the mountains of the West kept vigil on the horizon. They were alone on the roof of the world. She pointed to long strips of wood that were moving gently in the night.

"Isao told me that the *sotōba* indicate the names the deceased will use in the afterlife, but I think it's cruel, the idea that the dead could be deprived of the names their loved ones knew them by."

She waved her hand toward the snowy paths.

"But still," she added, "I must say I don't feel crucified by your cemeteries the way I do by ours."

"Are they so different?" asked Haru.

"Very different. In the West, cemeteries are places of death. Here I can always feel life around me, if that makes any sense."

He recalled his imaginings in Takayama regarding Maud's ancestors and his own.

"One day I told a story to a French woman I had just met. Like all the others, it was a story Keisuke had told me."

He fell silent, surprised at his own openness.

"And what happened?" asked Emmanuelle.

"I really don't know," he said. "Something happened, but I don't know what."

She looked at him.

"Tell me the story," she said.

He hesitated.

"Go on," she insisted, "it seems important, and I like stories."

Behind him, Shinnyo-dō was murmuring. At his feet, at the bottom of the steps, was the place where he'd learned of his daughter's existence.

"The story takes place at the imperial court," he began.

"No," she said, interrupting, "tell it to me the way you told it to her, with the same words."

His mind filled with the image of Maud in the bath, naked, white, and silent, while he desired her.

"In around the middle of the Heian period," he continued, "the dawns were stunningly beautiful. In the depths of the heavens, sprays of purple flowers were withering. Sometimes huge birds were caught in this burning light. At the imperial court there lived a lady, confined to her quarters. Her nobility had sealed her fate as a captive, and even the little garden adjacent to her room was forbidden to her. But to contemplate the dawn she knelt on the wood on the outside veranda, and every morning since the New Year, a fox cub had stolen into the garden. Before long, a heavy rain began to fall, lasting until the spring, and the lady begged her new friend to come and shelter with her under the roof of the veranda by the garden, where there were only a few winter camellias and a maple tree. There they became acquainted, in silence."

He looked at the Frenchwoman, who was looking at the distant mountains. Something was floating, something was trembling. Is it in me? In her? Around us? he wondered. She turned to him.

"Then, once they'd invented a shared language, to each other they said only the names of their dead," he concluded. And at the same time, Emmanuelle murmured, in unison, *the names of their dead*, just as the snow began to fall.

Thus, in November 1980, a Japanese man and a French woman, from their outpost on the roof of the world, watched the snow fall. They believed they were at the beginning of a long friendship; they didn't know they'd never see one another again, that this night would forever be their only night. The sky was peeling, shedding white flecks borne away on an invisible breeze. The city grew pale, then disappeared, leaving them alone with the dead for their sole companions.

"Did you know that story?" asked Haru.

"No," she said.

She caught a few snowflakes on the back of her hand.

"I guessed."

"I'd be curious to know how," he said.

"Stories speak to us, we don't know how they do it. And your friend Keisuke and I have something in common. We've both lost a child."

She smiled at him as if he were the one who needed consoling, and suddenly the thought that his daughter could disappear, and with her, the new bridge thrown between himself and his family—between the past and the future, between his ancestors and his destiny—chilled him to the bone.

"I can see your fear," said Emmanuelle. "Actually, that's the only burden I've been relieved of—the burden of fear. As for all the rest, the burden remains the same. That's strange, don't you think? You suffer less over time, but things don't necessarily get better for all that."

She smiled, again a sad, consoling smile.

"I'd like to go down these steps," she said. "I have a hunch they'll lead somewhere."

He smiled in turn and followed her. Their footsteps packed down the snow, they could feel it moving. The snowstorm was letting up, the darkness expanding. They reached the bottom, by the pathway where Haru had once vowed he would be buried, and Emmanuelle dreamily continued along that path. After a few steps, she paused by an empty spot, leaned over, and touched the snow with the palm of her hand.

"The last time I saw my little boy alive, he was sleeping," she said as she stood up again. "He'd been sick for a long time, and the only respite I had was when he managed to get some sleep. Then he looked like any other little boy, and I gave myself permission to dream that everything was fine. I'm grateful to whatever fate let him sleep calmly, because when he was awake, it was always a nightmare."

She motioned that she wanted to keep going, and they went along the walkway before turning right toward the esplanade by the temple of Kurodani. The stars had reappeared, and Haru thought they looked unusually bright.

"Who was that French woman?" she asked.

He didn't know what to say. All around them, the tutelary presence of the buildings and the cemeteries, the potency of the graves and the snow, held an undecipherable message.

"What Tomoo said earlier about the *butō* is valid for love, as well," said Emmanuelle. "Art and desire sound the depths of our darkness."

"Keisuke told me I don't know how to understand women, but maybe it's my own self I don't understand."

"We all have a shadow side that creates blind spots where we're hidden from ourselves."

They continued their walk toward the entrance to Shinnyo-dō, passing through the complex's temples and adjacent gardens.

Haru knew every path, every bamboo stalk, every maple tree that moon and snow had covered in quicksilver. They came to the great red torii that showed the way to the main temple. There was a sort of density to the air and, at the same time, a delightful lightness.

"I do this loop every week," he said.

"You're lucky. There are a lot of people on this hill, and I'm not just referring to the dead."

"How do you know they're good company?" he said with a laugh.

"I haven't felt this good in a long time," she replied.

She took his arm in friendship, and he led her to the great courtyard, glad of her affection.

"The last time I took this walk with Isao, there was the same fragrance of something deep and joyful," she said when they were standing before the great pagoda.

"So there can be joy in spite of absence?" he asked.

"Sorrow is everywhere, I can't get away from it. But sometimes, in a particular place, with particular company, I can become a different woman. I can breathe again. After that, unfortunately, I go back to my usual self."

They went around the temple and back to the steps that led to Tomoo's sailing ship. As Haru was about to say goodbye, Emmanuelle stopped him.

"That Frenchwoman," she said, "did she seem sad when you told her the story about the lady with the fox?"

He was surprised, nodded. Emmanuelle nodded in turn.

"She belongs to an order you must guard against," she said. "Perhaps it's for the best that your fates aren't linked."

She squeezed his arm and gave him a smile.

"Adieu, dear friend," she said, "I hope to see you again soon."

He walked home the way he had come. At Takenaka, he tossed a coin onto the altar, rang the bell, bowed, clapped his hands, laughed at himself. He nearly fell several times on the steps at Yoshida, which were slippery with snow and dark from the tall trees. When he came out of the forested enclave into the heart of the city, he went back through the silent campus, came to the bridge over the Kamo-gawa, and paused for a moment. Large gray herons were poised on the riverbanks, where wild grasses shone silver with moonlight. He saw again the gesture Emmanuelle had made, touching the snow in the cemetery, and the earlier one where she had gathered snowflakes—the palm and the back of her hand, he thought, but she didn't only touch the snow, she touched the ground, she touched matter. He wondered what her little boy's name was, and suddenly told himself that the next time he saw her he would tell her about Rose. The thought of sharing his secret eased a burden he hadn't known he had. He looked at the stars, awestruck once again by their brilliance. Are they my judges, too? he wondered, recalling the night in Takayama.

He went home and into the kitchen, where he made some strong coffee, then drank it facing the maple tree in the moonlight. Was it the lack of sleep—two nights in a trance in the company of his ancestors, then of his brothers, and the conversation with Emmanuelle Revers? In the play of light and shadow, of darkness and snow, a troubling truth was becoming apparent, where everything contained its opposite, every desire its very negation. His life, which, until then, had seemed clear to him, was revealing its deep ambiguities, the palm and the back of his hand opening and closing in a circle dance of successive attraction and repulsion. Like the perpetual loop of the closed *ensō*, that life was turning around an invisible pivot, bringing suffering and joy in turn. He heard the door to the vestibule slide open, and Sayoko came into the room, wearing a raincoat and a beige woolen dress, her loose hair pushed back by a black headband. She looked him up and down, stern, frowning, and he understood that she didn't like him to see her like that, didn't like the fact he'd made the coffee himself. The day was dawning, it was snowing again, the maple was shivering. Sayoko came back in, her hair now tied behind her neck, and she was carrying a tray with tea, rice, and grilled fish. He thanked her, and she went away again, taking short little steps.

When Sayoko Nishiwaki entered Haru's service not quite two years earlier, she was twenty-three years old, had a son who was three, a husband who was twenty-nine, and a procession of invisible companions. She lived not far from Shinnyo-dō, where her mother, a widow, had left her a little house across from the Hōnen-in. Like everywhere, it was freezing cold in winter; spring and autumn were mild but fleeting; and in summer, the heat was stifling. To compound the inconvenience, the proximity of the forested mountains brought its lot of good-natured insects: mosquitoes, cockroaches, spiders, and poisonous centipedes which, should they bite you, would leave you with a good three days of fever. To enter the house, you went through a wooden gate and a tiny courtyard overrun with ferns and heavenly bamboo. The interior was protected against the light—and who knows what else—by multiple shutters, on both sides of the windows. At four in the afternoon, they heard the gong from the temple and would look up and watch as the neighborhood came to life. There were tiny shops everywhere, selling tofu, fresh coffee, mochi, and homemade miso. Life was insignificant and intense, regular as clockwork, shot through with bursts of folly. They enjoyed the protection of their small perimeter of hills embedded in the wider district. They all knew one another and kept an eye on one another, and what the shutters hid, the neighborhood's organic cohesion could see.

It was there that Sayoko was brought up by her mother. On weekdays, Masako worked at a traditional inn near the foot of the Yoshida hill, a luxury establishment run by an old family who were somewhat strapped for cash. They welcomed distinguished guests, eminent Japanese leaders, and a few foreigners in Kyōto on business. Masako helped out in the kitchen, the dining room, and the bedrooms, wore her kimono, and learned how to keep the register and the accounts books. The place was a combination of authentic Japanese style and the Western influences characteristic of the Meiji period, where the décor was typified by art nouveau and a leaning toward a British atmosphere. There were magnificent gardens all around, with azaleas, maples, and pine trees pruned by quality gardeners. After school, Sayoko joined her mother there, and from her she learned the basics of running a top-end establishment. How to adjust and wear a kimono, how to kneel, how to greet, cook, keep the books. She learned the guests' rank, the ways of foreigners, and the whims of human beings. At Yoshida Honkan, Sayoko learned how to serve.

The encounter between her own constitution and this world of work and tradition endowed Sayoko with a nature that was both pragmatic and whimsical. Regarding the latter, she liked nothing better than to frequent places where she might hear what the spirits were murmuring. She went to the Buddhist temple of Hōnen-in that was across the street from her mother's house and, near the *ryokan*, to the Shinto shrine in Yoshida, the oldest in the city. There she would spend a long time by the altar at Takenaka, where she came up with a hybrid theory regarding divinities and *kami*, informed by the declarations of monks and priests and by her own childish suppositions. As a woman, she did not change; if anything, she invested even more passion into this practice than before. This led to conversations where her sense of organization dominated, then suddenly her train of thought would derail. In fact, she held a conception of spirits from both religions that belonged to her alone, and which explained, in part, her incongruous transformations: the *kami*—or who knows who else—would whisper words to her that others could not hear. Other than that, she was slim, smooth, supple, and obstinate, smiled rarely, controlled everything, applied fervor to her care. Life was a passage in which work must be done seriously; she eschewed any penchant for pleasure, and she displayed a sort of ingenuousness that—as Keisuke would assert one day—verged on the sublime.

After secondary school, encouraged by Hirai-san, the owner of the *ryokan*, she went to study art history in Nara. Her mother died suddenly that summer, and Sayoko inherited a little nest egg she then earmarked for her studies. Her three sisters from her mother's first marriage, who were older, lived in the Tōkyō region. Sayoko rented out the house in Kyōto and went to stay in Nara with a cousin on her father's side. At the end of the day, her mind silky with knowledge and works of art, she would walk home along the rear side of the Grand Temple. One evening, without warning, she felt afraid. She saw before her the vastness of art and the shadows the buildings cast on the ground like so many threats. The darkened outline of the temple, massive and full of reproach, stared down at her, and she was overcome by a shapeless terror. She took a few steps, and the elongated reflections cast by the lanterns terrified her. She knelt on the stone path and thought: How dare you? She got back to her feet, bowed, and fled. The very next day she went back to Kyōto, and three months later she was married.

After her life as a child, her life at the *ryokan*, then in Nara, came her life as wife and mother: unsurprisingly, she only lasted three years. On January 1, 1979, at dawn—her son and husband were still sleeping—she left the house, set off down the Path of Philosophy, passed beneath the snow-covered cherry trees, continued west along the deserted streets and came to the foot of Shinnyo-dō, where she paused for a moment. She heard cracking noises and tiny sounds, the sky was white, ravens circled above the gray roofs. She continued along the path of her destiny, climbed the hill, walked through the temple enclosure and then back down to the *ryokan*. There she went in through the service entrance, continued along the corridor, and found Hirai-san at her low table, writing a poem with brush and ink.

"Ah, is it you, Sayoko?" the old lady said affectionately. "To what do I owe the honor of this early morning visit? The new year?"

"I'd like to work for you," Sayoko replied, after greeting her respectfully.

Bowing deeply, she added, "The way my mother did."

Hirai-san gingerly put down her brush and gave a sigh.

"We miss Masako very much," she said, "so very much."

She motioned to Sayoko to sit down.

"But you're not cut out for this work," she said.

Sayoko began to protest, and Hirai-san raised her hand.

"You always have astonishing premonitions, and you haven't come here by chance. Hasegawa-san paid me a neighborly visit last night."

She stood up and went to fetch a piece of paper from her desk.

"Call this number. One of his friends, a gentleman you can trust, is looking for a housekeeper."

She sat back down and picked up her brush, but as Sayoko was about to go out, she called her back and said, "This will be your first kingdom."

The next day, Sayoko made a phone call, left her son with a neighbor, and went to visit her first kingdom. When she came home, she found her husband in the little courtyard, already back from work.

"I was worried," he said.

"I was hired right away," she said. "It's for a respectable gentleman."

"You've been hired?" he echoed.

"The house is by the Kamo-gawa," she said, "it's a very beautiful house, in fact."

He was used to the way she suddenly changed the subject, and, adapting to the new situation, he asked, "What will you be doing, exactly?"

"Everything," she answered, and that was how she began her new life.

Every morning she went to find the light in her second home—which, in fact, was her true home, the place of all her past lives and lives to come, just as Shinnyo-dō was for Haru. She knew that her initial wonder would not fade, that with each dawn she would relive the same enchantment of wood and foliage, the same sensation that everything was exact, pure, and right—just as it should be. The house by the river incorporated the elements she revered in art, but it also offered her a fitting domain, where she had her place and could reign free of danger. And in addition, she had liked Haru immediately and vowed to take care of him until the end, with a devotion that, later on, would strike some people as fanatical. Finally, not long after her enthronement in her kingdom, the last of her epiphanies occurred. During her first days, she examined the walls and the works of art, she listened to the house, questioned the tree, and, puzzled, came to realize that something was missing. She walked up and down the corridors, around the rooms, with the awareness of a ghostly presence. She was trying to find something but didn't know what. And then, two weeks after going into service, early one morning in January, she met Keisuke.

She opened the door to him, and he collapsed in her arms, his breath fetid, his shirt hanging out, one shoe missing. She pushed him away, and he slumped limply onto the floor in the vestibule. Dazed, she looked at him, then turned to Haru, who had followed him in, and said, "Is this man a prince?"

Haru studied Keisuke—hairy and untidy, giggling moronically.

"A prince?" he said.

But she wasn't listening, and, ecstatic, she leaned over the drunkard. Now she understood: what she'd been looking for these last two weeks lived outside the house, and yet he incarnated it.

"I'll go make some coffee," she said with a smile.

What came next was a fantastical dialogue. Haru had managed to drag Keisuke into the main room and to prop him up, his behind on a cushion, his back against the maple tree cage. Sayoko came in with the coffee and knelt before them, her hands folded over her black obi with its embroidery of yellow chrysanthemums. After a first cup, Keisuke began nodding his head unsteadily.

"Oh, those big chrysanthemums," he chirped, his eyes tearful.

"Did she like them very much?" asked Sayoko.

"She did," said Keisuke.

Sayoko tilted her head, seemed to be listening to something or someone.

"Ah," she said sadly, "your little girl, too!"

"My little girl, too," Keisuke intoned.

"She loved flowers, like her mother?"

"Like her mother," said Keisuke.

Sayoko lowered her gaze, sorrowfully.

She poured him a second cup of coffee. He drank it in one gulp.

"Who are you?" he asked, trying to adjust his vision, frowning, squinting.

Apparently he didn't succeed, as he went on to exclaim, "A fox! A fox in a kimono! Oh, the lovely chrysanthemums!"

He pointed at Haru.

"This man here," he said to Sayoko, "this man here is a samurai and an esthete in the body of a tradesman. He knows tea, he knows the spirit, he knows business."

Sayoko nodded primly.

"But he doesn't understand women at all," said Keisuke. "He looks at them, but he doesn't see them. He examines the merchandise and counts in units of flesh. The only thing that'll save him, in the end, is that he doesn't like straight lines."

He laughed and tried unsuccessfully to stand up.

"Mountain people are real dumbasses," he declared, "but when everything's collapsing around you, they're the sort of imbecile you want by your side."

Then, surprised, he exclaimed, "Oh, but hang on a minute, you're not a fox?"

Sayoko shook her head.

"I don't think so," she said, and, shattering all rules of propriety, decorum, and feminine reserve, she added, "This is your home."

The rest of that morning went by with the potter snoring and drooling on the low sofa in the main room, Sayoko watching over her new hero with the jealous vigilance of a mother wolf, and Haru dealing with some business and meditating in his study. At the beginning of the afternoon, Keisuke emerged from his coma, and he found, within arm's reach, some strong tea and a little bowl of nattō.

"Your housekeeper is clairvoyant," he said to Haru, who was reading and smoking nearby.

"Maybe she listens to the stars," suggested Haru.

"You don't realize what you're saying," said Keisuke, amused.

"I may be a mountain yokel, but I can hear the stars."

On impulse, he recited the lines from the poem from Kakurezato, and silence fell.

"It's by Setsuko Nozawa," said Keisuke eventually.

After another pause he added, "Sae liked her very much."

"She's still alive?" asked Haru.

"The dead are alive," said Keisuke, "since they live through us."

"I mean the poetess," said Haru.

"I know," said Keisuke, "but I like to remind you of the things that matter. For example: the true language of Japan, the language of the stars, was invented by women of letters during the Heian period, a language that spoke of rain, snow, the night, and a hundred different ways of feeling, with a richness and sensibility that modernity has obliterated. Everything that is alive in Japan comes from the way of women."

He waved his nattō under Haru's nose.

"Women are our judges. I don't know what you're up to, but you'd do better not to forget it."

And now, one year later, the memory of Keisuke's words mingled with those he'd heard the night before, from Emmanuelle Revers: *She belongs to an order you must guard against.* Haru laughed, confounded by the intrigues of fate. The stars had guided him to his ancestors and then to his brothers, and now they were showing him his judges. Their names were Sayoko, Emmanuelle, and Paule, the kindly tutors of a child whose destiny was the responsibility of women. He liked the fact that Sayoko knew about Rose, he planned to confide in Emmanuelle, and he was putting Rose's fate into Paule's hands. All three had the same dreaming intelligence, the same talent for the invisible, the same intense presence that made them a beneficial community for his daughter. Maud, on the other hand, and all her hostile order, must leave Rose's life forever. He removed all the photographs where she appeared from his files and the wooden panels in his study, and he called Manabu Umebayashi and asked him to relay his request to the French photographer. Finally, he did what the tribunal of his benefactresses seemed quite naturally to suggest: he spoke to Sayoko.

He spoke to her the next day in private, by the maple tree cage. She brought some tea and sat down across from him.

"Rose's mother does not want me to have any part in my daughter's life," he said.

"The sad Frenchwoman," said Sayoko.

"You remember her?"

"I passed her in the vestibule one morning," she said. "She was wearing a green dress."

She clasped and re-clasped her hands.

"She was very beautiful, and very sad," she added.

"Precisely," said Haru, "I'm at a loss for how to deal with such sadness."

"It's a malediction, a *tatari*," she said. "A very powerful *kami*, or maybe a *yōkai*, because I can see a fox. Is it a good or a bad spirit, that's what has to be determined."

She frowned.

"In the old days, foxes and humans lived side by side," she continued, "so it's hard to know. To act, you have to find the cause of her sadness, but she's gone back to France. How do the French purify themselves? If this is a cycle, it has to be broken right away."

"How can I be close to my daughter if I'm absent from her life?" he asked.

"Close?" she echoed, as if it were a dirty word. "It's better to be absent."

He was taken aback.

"I don't understand."

"Distance preserves the bond," she said. "Reality destroys it."

"But love requires a certain closeness," he protested.

She laughed.

"You will give," she said. "You will give like the stars that watch over us, without expecting anything in return."

He was surprised by this entrance of stars onto a stage already crowded with foxes and spirits, and suspected that Sayoko and Keisuke had been talking behind his back.

"And what you cannot do with a woman, you can do with a child," she added, getting to her feet.

He spent the rest of the morning thinking about what she'd said. He recalled the major events of the year gone by and felt a resolve strengthen inside him. Keisuke had said the only thing that would save him in the end was that he didn't like straight lines. Today, with the guidance of foxes and stars, he could hear their message. Perhaps he could only be a father in the way of an *ensō* or a calligraphy, where the curves and blockages of his inner self were reflected. His business acumen, his talent for success, his love of women and seduction, his incompetence at intimacy went some way, perhaps, toward explaining his desire for Maud and his readiness to love a child he couldn't approach in a straight line. Also, what was the solution for that incompetence? Through Sayoko's words, Rose was offering him the chance to fulfill an innate aspiration, that of doing something neither the tradesman nor the lover could do: because, deep down, he wanted to give. He realized this, accepted it, regarded it with joy. He made it the stuff of his identity as a father, and elevated it to the highest point of his conscience. He would give. He would give without taking the straight path, but he would give all the same. And if, all along that path of giving, he honored his family, loved his brothers, and followed the way of women, he might learn how to become a father. *The way of women*, he said to himself again, the way he habitually said, *the way of tea*, and he placed his fate in the hands of his judges.

A Long Time

And so years went by, devoted to honoring the way of women, to dreading the cycle of malediction, and to conversing with an absent child, the only form of gift Haru had available to him then. Every morning, he got up, greeted his river and his mountains, drank a cup of tea, conversed with Rose, lit a cigarette, and began his workday. In the evening in his bath, like every conscientious father, he resumed the conversation he'd begun that morning. In fact, he doubted many fathers showed this much interest in their daughters. Maud's threat had taken Rose away from him but afforded him a space of freedom that few of his peers enjoyed or actually wanted. Children were a woman's domain, and, with the exception of Keisuke, Haru did not know a single Japanese man who thrilled to the prospect of raising his children.

He observed with particular interest the way Beth was bringing up her son. He still saw her often, slept with her, talked business with her. Their friendship was fluid, with nothing romantic at stake, but in terms of sex, they had everything they needed for mutual satisfaction. Moreover, if Beth remained something of a mystery to Haru, it was, unlike with Maud, a mystery that did not leave him blind. She was only partially opaque to him—and all the more desirable—because she was English, but apart from that, they were alike in many ways. She often brought William with her to lunch with Haru and after a while it became a ritual: every Friday, the three of them met up at Mishima Tei on Teramachi, in the covered shopping arcade in the center of town. It was an old establishment, located in a former *machiya*, where they served sukiyaki that William adored. The child sitting opposite Haru was gentle and silent, with big blue eyes and long dark lashes. He had inherited his mother's fine bone structure and his father's dark hair, small nose, and Japanese complexion. Tall, delicate, and strange, he was so beautiful that passersby would turn around in the street to look at him. Beth and Haru celebrated his twelfth birthday watching him stuff himself with thinly sliced Wagyu beef cooked in sake and sugar and dipped in raw egg. Haru liked to see how caring she was as a mother, for all that she disliked any form of loving sentiment. All she wanted was a man's body for sex and the power to build empires. As for the rest, she divided her time between her linked love for her son and for Zen gardens.

Beth Scott—that was her maiden name—had loved Japan from the moment she set her eyes on the sand at Nanzen-ji and had, from the first moment, as well, loved the child born of her passion for Japan. Haru was always stunned when he thought of her choice of husband; he'd crossed paths with him at certain business events and barely noticed him: a man devoid of any appreciable qualities. But he knew that Ryū Nakamura, after his first night with Beth, had said to her, I will give you Japan, a comfortable life, and children, if you want them. In return, you will be free, but you'll remain my partner forever. And, what's more, it wasn't fair to say he was devoid of any qualities, or to believe that Beth Scott was devoid of any attachment. There were few people she liked, but where others were driven by emotional impulses, she was driven by esteem and respect. Her husband admired her for this, and consequently, within the first two years of their marriage, the revenues of his real estate business had increased five-fold. No one was fooled, but she played the game of appearances, keeping quiet while exerting power behind the throne. The Japanese may not have liked her, but they respected her, and respect was all she herself gave to others, or expected of them.

There had been two moments in Beth's life, however, when she escaped her own self-control. The day she turned twenty-two, she found herself standing for the first time before the main garden at Nanzen-ji. It was raining, and she had paid at the entrance to the temple, taken her shoes off, and gone down a long dark corridor until the scene emerged in the light before her. The ten thousand kilometers she had come, some vague intuitions, the longings she could not put into words: everything began to make sense in the form of a garden where there were rocks, moss, a few camellias, one or two azaleas, four trees, and a sea of sand raked with waves. To her left and in front of her were walls lined with white and topped with gray tiles; to her right, a long external gallery, part of the temple; in the distance, the roofs of other temples, the tree-covered mountains, and the sky above the crests. Everywhere, the sound of rain. In Beth, a dry, desolate strand had been reshaped into a landscape of solitude, a spirit cleansed of pain. Contemplating the garden and seeing her own inner vista refracted and appeased, she thought, Here, I can confront anything. And later, on the same day in the spring of 1969, when she turned twenty-four, she found herself gazing at her second private landscape. The sensation was identical: the invisible despair rooted inside her came into the light and was transformed into joy, obeying the same transformative power she had felt in the garden at the temple. But when Ryū came to the maternity ward to make the acquaintance of his son, she said:

"His name is William."

"He must have a Japanese name, too," said Ryū.

"As you like," she said, "but we'll only call him William."

Twelve years later to the day, Haru was together with

William and Beth in the old *machiya* on Teramachi, where the sighs and splendor of a century of history lay hidden in the cracks in the paper partitioning walls. He liked the fact that Beth was a mother who did not expect her son to make her exist in return, and it filled him with wonder to see her give her love so unreservedly. They were having lunch in a private room where a hostess had left them with a stove, a cast iron nabe, slices of beef, chrysanthemum leaves, chives, onions, mushrooms, tofu, and a beaten raw egg. It was a sweet time. The wood creaked. Spirits whispered. The roof structure of the old building spoke of the joys and woes of the century gone by, the perennial nature of culture, its ability to adapt and not die. Outside was the covered arcade with its flashy boutiques, neon signs, blaring music, and dirty concrete. Here, these doors that diners slid open and closed had known three Imperial eras.

At one point, toward the end of the meal, Haru turned to look at William. The boy was staring at him with unusual intensity, his eyes open wide, filled with a dark terror, and in that ink-drowned gaze Haru saw the silhouette of a ghost slip by. The boy looked down, his anguish disappeared, and Haru helped himself to sake, to banish his unease. Beth hadn't noticed.

"We're happy here," she said. "Ten years in Tōkyō wasn't such a long purgatory, but still, it was time to leave."

William nibbled on his mushrooms and cooked his cubes of tofu, humming. Haru told Beth that he wanted to buy an apartment in Tōkyō. He was tired of staying in hotels, and his business there was doing well.

"Let's go visit a few together next week," she said, as she stroked her son's hair.

Yet again, a spectral fear in the boy's irises, yet again, Beth was smiling, unseeing, completely absorbed in her affection for her son. What's going on? Haru wondered, his throat tight, thinking of Rose. Can shadows come so quickly into a child's heart? He suddenly pictured himself as he'd been at that age, on the bank of his torrent, and that fleeting vision tinged with sadness, silence, and shadows filled him with a lurking dread.

F our years went by, however, and nothing fateful happened. During those four years, Haru went on talking to his daughter, reassuring himself that the cycle of malediction was a mirage, and when it came to his decisions, he went on placing his trust in women.

The photographs and reports came from France every three months: Rose was growing, and Haru scrutinized the features of the laughing little redhead, his rapture mixed with wonder. Nothing about her suggested she had a Japanese father, and, other than the color of her eyes and hair, she didn't look like her mother, either. She had freckles, a mischievous upturned nose, a smooth oval face, and a high flat forehead, whereas Maud's was narrow and somewhat prominent. In one of the photographs, he saw her wrapped in a little orange coat, with a green beanie pulled down to her brows, wisps of red locks around her cheeks, her expression lively and cheerful and set on happiness. She seemed such a denial of any foreshadowing of malediction that he looked at the picture every day, as if rubbing a talisman with his hand. In another picture, her face was turned up as she gazed intensely at her grandmother, and Haru was surprised to see himself in her, beyond the distance of continents and despite the trials set by fate. She had that same charm born of the union between fervor and lightness that he knew himself to possess. She x-rayed life as eagerly as he had as a boy. In the same way that his childhood self had come into the world, to devour it, she observed, dissected, desired everything. Paule, by her side, was clapping her hands, smiling, singing and speaking to her granddaughter with a delight that was so contagious that sometimes, when he saw one of the photographs for the first time, Haru laughed out loud. It reassured him to know that his daughter's fate rested in Paule's hands—all the more so in that, while Maud might no longer be featured in the pictures, reports had confirmed that she sat in the sun room all day long, weeping intermittently. But Rose was alive and vibrant, and Haru went on speaking to her morning and night—about his river, his brothers, and his distant ancestors. He told her all about Takayama and Kyōto, the mountains here, and the mountains there, the stages involved in fermenting sake, the importance of foxes. He explained his work to her and shared his likes and dislikes, unveiled the workings—and tricks—of his trade. As he did so, he got to know himself in a way he never had before—many-sided, complex, linked to the galaxy of his forefathers. Finally, he lit a cigarette, and returned to his Japanese life.

With a relative sense of balance, life bustled along until the year of the great beginning. Business was flourishing, so with Beth's help Haru bought a large apartment in Tōkyō. He went there two or three times a month, organized press lunches, ephemeral exhibitions, and parties at the house of a friend who owned an apartment block in Ginza. There he met women, men who became his friends, and all sorts of people who added significantly to his network. He spent studious and festive days there and was doing marvelously well. But when he came back to Kyōto, back to his home, his temples and his mountains, he felt reborn. Gilded with success, he went looking for the man he'd once been, before the art dealer. He entered the house by the Kamo-gawa and came back out to go find his friends. He spotted Keisuke at the back of a bar and knew he was at the pulsing center of his life.

From time to time, he exchanged letters with Emmanuelle Revers, in the hopes that she might come back to Japan and give him a chance to tell her about Rose. Three years after their first meeting, she wrote to say she would be giving a series of recitals in the spring in Nagoya and Tōkyō. But I'll come and see you in Kyōto, she said at the end of the letter, and we'll walk together under the cherry trees at Shinnyo-dō. After that, he had no more news from her until, through Tomoo, he heard that the concerts had been canceled. A week later, he received a letter, its trembling handwriting difficult to decipher. I'm ill, she explained, and I know, whatever the doctors may say, that it will be fatal. He wrote back that she was surely mistaken, that he was thinking about her, and that she would soon return to Japan. In her reply, she thanked him and added: I'm not worried about dying, but when I'm no longer here, who will remember my little boy? After that, he had no more news at all. He grew worried and called Manabu Umebayashi, who told him that Emmanuelle Revers no longer left the house and no longer received visitors. Finally, one day, when no one had seen the storm coming, the year 1985 arrived, and with it the beginning of everything that had been foretold.

1985—the year of four deaths. Haru learned of the first one from Tomoo on the afternoon of January 3. He had not planned to go to Shinnyo-dō that day, but a last-minute impulse drove him out into the snow. He hailed a cab and was dropped off outside the sailing ship just as night was falling. Tomoo greeted him and said, Emmanuelle Revers has died, and he added, Isao is ill. What do you mean, ill? asked Haru, but Tomoo didn't say, brought him inside and led him to the room of parties and sake. There, his only love lay across an armchair, in great pain. His cheeks were hollow, his eyes dull, and he was having difficulty breathing. His beautiful face, full of youth only the day before, had been overtaken by age. He was ill for a week and then died. Friends came one after the other to the hospital, Tomoo never left his side, but there was nothing to be done; they could only watch as he faded away. On the morning of January 10, Haru went into the hospital room and found Tomoo kneeling on the floor, his eyes closed, his hands on his thighs. He knelt down beside him, and they stayed there together in the pseudo-silence of the medical monitors, then stood up and saw that Isao was dead. Tomoo did not flinch, did not weep, did not speak, and Haru followed his example. They stood looking at the young man's tortured body—he who had been so handsome, so joyful—until a nurse came in, then the doctor, and others still, so they left the room.

The funeral wake was held at the home of Isao's parents in Arashiyama, the other side of town. The monk was senile and indifferent, reciting the sutra in a droning voice; the place was sinister, the family silent and reproachful, and no one knew whether it was because of the death or because Isao's friends were there. The house overlooked the river Katsura, in a spot where it was wide and full of stones: it resembled an expanse of moon. The garden was poorly kept, dark, and humid. Everything emanated pettiness and boredom. The visitors presented their envelopes of offerings, while Isao, his features unrecognizable, lay in the middle of that swamp. The funeral the following day was no different, and Tomoo, doing what was expected of him, attended in the role of the deceased's flatmate. He placed a flower in the open coffin and went away without looking back. That same evening, a sizeable crowd gathered at Shinnyo-dō.

His lifelong friends were there, and colleagues from the theater where Isao had been stage manager. An astronomical amount of sake was drunk. One of his brothers, the only one Tomoo had ever spent time with, joined them just as the alternating cycles of drinking and speeches began—and looked set to last all night. They drank, someone got up and spoke, they drank some more, someone else got up and spoke in turn. Tomoo, sprawled in the armchair where the love of his life had known so much pain, listened to them all, not drinking. The actors and technicians shared anecdotes from the stage, friends shared anecdotes of friendship, and all were drunk on sake and sorrow. At one point, Keisuke turned to Isao's brother.

"Well then, Ieyasu, do you believe in the ideal life?"

The brother, of course, was too drunk to reply.

"It doesn't exist," said Keisuke. "Don't judge your parents and brothers too harshly: they believe in what they've been told to do rather than doing what they believe in, like so many people. But Isao only believed in humanity, and, because of that, he was one of those men with whom an ideal life is possible."

There were some murmurs of agreement, and Tomoo finally drank four cups in a row. At around ten, there was a ring at the door of the sailing ship: it was Jacques Melland, together with a very young man wearing the same black ascot as his father. He offered his condolences to Tomoo in Japanese and said, pointing to his son, "I'd like him to learn."

The boy introduced himself in hesitant Japanese. His name was Édouard, he was glad to meet them, and he added, in English, that he was sorry about Isao.

"How old are you?" asked Tomoo.

"Sixteen," he replied.

Through the window, below the lamp post, the cherry tree could be seen, lacquered with winter and darkness. As the hours passed, some guests fell asleep on the tatami, others left, and at one point, the only ones still talking and drinking were the two Frenchmen and the trio of Japanese friends. At first, they made an effort to speak English, but with the help of the sake they reverted to Japanese, and Haru, the only one who was still up to it, translated for Jacques—who understood fairly well—and Édouard—who understood nothing at all. Even Tomoo was beginning to struggle, and at around midnight, he had to ask Jacques to repeat his question twice over, regarding Isao's death.

"A short illness," he replied, once he understood. "Hell is right nearby; you can fall into it while going through a fogbank."

Keisuke, who had been snoring in little bursts, raised his head.

"Hell?" he said. "I only lived for one hour, and yet I'm not allowed to die. I'm destined to outlive the people I love, so I'm sitting here like a stupid bastard waiting for all of you to die."

He burped and refilled his cup.

"But you," he added, looking at Tomoo, "you're destined for other things."

Haru translated for Jacques and Édouard.

"Ah," said Jacques, "that's what I thought you said. Personally, I will die before my loved ones, but the hour has already passed, and all that's left to do is kill time."

He turned to his son.

"I love you," he said, "but, you see, I'm talking about my life as a man."

"Why is Tomoo destined for other things?" asked Édouard.

Haru put the question to Keisuke in Japanese.

"Tochan?" said Keisuke. "He's lucky, that's all. He'll have other loves in his life."

"Are you a master of luck?" asked Édouard.

"Of course," said Keisuke.

"Can you tell me if I'm lucky?"

Keisuke laughed.

"I'm not a medium," he said, "I can't see just because someone orders me to."

"Then what are you?" asked Édouard.

"A poet," said Keisuke.

After that, the evening went by quickly, with no one really able to keep up the conversation. Haru alone went on talking with Édouard.

"Do you know what you want to do with your life?" he asked.

"I'm going to take over the shop," said Édouard. "But first I'll study art and Asian languages."

"Do you like business?" asked Haru.

"Oh," said Édouard, "not really, but it's a means, after all."

"A means to what?"

"To be here," he replied.

He looked around the room.

"I never thought that one day I'd actually understand something about my father."

And, pointing at Tomoo, "I would also never have suspected

that my father could understand me. Clearly we live on different planets, except when we're in Japan."

"That's not such a bad thing," said Haru. Then, in a more casual tone: "Do you know our mutual friend, Maud Arden?"

"Maud? She had a daughter and went and shut herself away at her mother's place. My father likes her, I don't really know why. I think she's crazy. To be honest, I feel sorry for her daughter."

"Crazy?" said Haru.

"What I mean is—who besides monks and crazy people goes and leaves the world behind at the age of thirty?"

At three in the morning, Jacques and Édouard took their leave. Keisuke was snoring on the tatami along with a few other guests, and Tomoo was resting in his armchair, his eyes half-closed. Haru went out into the cold night and up the steps toward the temple. The sky was clear, the stone lanterns cast long slender shadows on the courtyard, the gravel sparkled. What Édouard had said to him—in Japan, my father and I understand each other—gave Haru a new perspective on his relationship with his daughter. He wanted to give, and until tonight, he had thought that consisted in speaking to Rose and, later on, in leaving his property to her. Now the idea made him laugh; a little cloud of vapor rose from his lips. Heading toward Kurodani, he wove his way between the gravestones until he reached the top of the great stairway. A faint rumbling along with the shriek of sirens rose from the city below him. To his left, in the distance, he could see the observation tower, the tallest building in a city that had been spared any skyscrapers, a tower that looked oddly like a steel mushroom, with its white base and bright red circular platform. In the middle, the windows of the Hotel Okura, the second-tallest building in Kyōto, sent little halos of light into the faint mist. In the distance, on the right-hand side, lapping against the sheer face of the mountains, was an expanse of buildings that were part of the new city. Here and there, lost amid the ocean of concrete, the roof of a temple stood out like a beacon. Everything else was bathed in a neon aura. Haru stood for a long time gazing out at the blend of ugliness and grace.

As it happened, his thirty-six-year-old self was devoted to the task of understanding the living, because all around him, human beings were dying, and he had to take care of those who were still there.

The third person to take their leave, after Emmanuelle and Isao, was Beth's husband Ryū Nakamura, at the age of forty. At around noon on January 20—which happened to be Haru's birthday—he collapsed on the ground at a building site, and the emergency services could do nothing more than certify his death. Beth was waiting for him at a nearby restaurant, where they were meant to meet for lunch. She saw Ryū's right-hand man coming toward her, and the blood drained from her face to settle in her feet. When he said, "Nakamura-san has had an attack," she slumped back on her chair in the embrace of infinite relief, and a few days later she said to Haru, "I thought it was William." The funeral was impressive, and Beth went to great pains to satisfy Japanese opinion by conforming to tradition, paying sincere homage to her husband and preparing the future of the company. William was silent, in the same way he was silent during their lunches on Teramachi and in life in general. He was so beautiful that his beauty was heartbreaking; everyone dreaded it might be shattered someday, the way one dreads such a fate befalling any perfect work of art. There were still times when his gaze turned somber, but Haru had gotten used to it; none of his expressions came close to that terror-stricken look he had witnessed on the day the boy turned twelve. With adolescence, his deep blue eyes had acquired a crystalline texture, and it was as if intensity, at its most extreme, had become transparency. His tall physique, his black hair, his pale white skin added a singular elegance to his beauty, which continued to fascinate passersby. But William himself, whatever the occasion, remained impassive and silent, and seemed neither to hear nor to see anyone but his mother. He spoke English with her, although during their lunches at Mishima Tei, he also spoke Japanese. Haru had noticed that he didn't seem as sad when he spoke the language of his father, and at the funeral he looked, to Haru, more at ease in his Japanese skin than he ever had in his British clothing. Still, regardless of the idiom, William remained a mystery.

A few days went by with no further blows. Then came February 13, and in mid-afternoon Sayoko said, "There's something strange in the air." That evening, Haru had dinner with Keisuke and Tomoo in a soba restaurant on Shirakawa, the major artery below the sailing ship. There they drank within reason, and then they went to amend that half-measure in a bar in the city center that served French wine, the first of its kind in Kyōto. "Meh," said Keisuke, after a glass of Burgundy that cost an arm and a leg. They ordered a vintage Bordeaux, which they sipped, bobbing their heads from side to side—"It doesn't come close to a good sake," said Keisuke in the end— and they moved on to one of their favorite bars, which served equally pricey rare sake. After two festive hours, Haru had a sudden sensation that he attributed to the alcohol: the world was receding, like the sea from the shore before a tsunami. He saw streets and buildings sucked up into an invisible vortex and borne far away, and he could not hold them back. At that same moment Keisuke, talking about Tarō, his eldest boy, said: "He's gone diving in Okinawa, young people nowadays are nuts, when I was his age I went looking for raku earth in the mountains." Tomoo took a taxi to Shinnyo-dō, and Keisuke and Haru walked back to the house by the Kamo-gawa. Haru felt rather the worse for wear, but he could walk in a straight line and wasn't slurring his words. He held Keisuke and hauled him as far as the low sofa in the main room, where he deposited him before going to his bedroom.

He woke up to rain and an awareness that something was wrong. In the maple room, Sayoko was planning her shopping while she watched Keisuke out of the corner of her eye. He was snoring, his head rammed into a pillow, one leg dangling, the other one half-uncovered with his trouser leg pushed up to his knee. In the rain, the mountains of the East disappeared behind continual volleys of fog. The doorbell rang, Sayoko went to the vestibule and came back with her arms filled with cherry branches. Haru watched her arrange them in a tall clay vase with grooved sides. Her gestures were surgical, without the slightest hesitancy, ordered—as was everything she did—by the inspiration of millennial wisdom. She finished her arrangement, and Keisuke opened his eyes and exclaimed, "Ah, that vase isn't bad!"

Haru laughed.

"Neither is the potter who made it."

"Is it one of mine?"

"It's one of yours."

They had a chat while drinking their tea and smoking. At around eleven o'clock, Sayoko, who was coming and going around the house, paused by the picture window that looked out toward the river. She seemed to be searching the gray magma of the landscape, and she held one hand to her chest.

"Is everything all right?" asked Haru.

"I don't know," she said.

He stood up, worried.

"No," she said, "I'm all right."

Haru and Keisuke exchanged a glance.

"I don't like this," said Keisuke, "you know she's clairvoyant."

"You make fun of religion, and you believe in clairvoyance?" said Haru with a chuckle.

"I believe in human beings and their talents," said Keisuke.

They left the house at around noon, and Haru went to catch the train to Tōkyō. The late afternoon was spent in business meetings, and that evening he hosted a well-watered dinner, where one of the most important sales of his career was finalized. He got back to the apartment in Hongō at around 3 A.M. The telephone was ringing. He picked up the receiver and heard Sayoko say, "Tarō-san has been killed." "Killed?" he repeated, not understanding. "In Okinawa, on Zamami Island," she said. "A diving accident." Her voice was cold, robotic. After a silence, she added, "I should have known." "You couldn't have known," said Haru and, after another pause, "I'll get the next train."

He caught the five o'clock Shinkansen and was home before eight. Sayoko opened the door to him. In the maple tree room, he found Keisuke, sitting with his back against the glass cage.

"To die on Zamami at the age of sixteen: fate really excels at cruelty," said the potter.

Haru sat down next to him.

"That was where I fell in love with Sae."

He took the cigarette Haru held out to him.

"Fate is killing all her branches," he continued. "What will you find this time to console me?"

Haru didn't answer.

"They're bringing the body back today," continued Keisuke. "Nobu will get here this morning. It's a beautiful place, you know, the beach at Furuzamami."

He took a long drag on his cigarette.

"The worst of it," he said, "is that I'm going to have to put up with those monks again. Incense, monks, sutras, lamebrained offerings in pretty envelopes, and then more monks."

At the wake, Keisuke's brother Hiroshi officiated with dignity. A huge crowd attended the funeral the following day— "They've come here for you, for Nobu, for Tarō, for Sae, and for Yōko," Haru said to Keisuke. His potter friend gave him a blank look, then began sobbing with such wrenching despair that Haru led him to one side, out of sight of his last son, and he wept for a long time in the silence of their friendship. At the end of the funeral, he addressed the mourners, and in keeping with tradition, he thanked them for being there. His eyes were dry, his shoulders rounded, and he spoke gently as he looked at Nobu, the only surviving sibling.

"As long as you are here, I will want to live, because although absence is crushing me, your presence fills me with joy," he said. "I want you to know that if I were alone, I would call on the powers of death and say, I'm not afraid of you. But I'm not alone, and if life has only one hour of fervor left to offer me, I want us to spend it together."

One evening a few days later, Haru, Tomoo, and Keisuke got together at the Shinnyo-dō sailing ship. Tomoo served them sake, and while they drank, they nibbled senbei. There was silence; all that could be heard was the munching of crackers and the sound of their cups being placed on the table. After an hour, Tomoo stood up and went to put a record on the turntable.

"Ella Fitzgerald and Joe Pass," he said. "The song was written by eden ahbez. Years later he lost his son Tatha, who drowned at the age of twenty-two."

They listened to the piece. Haru repeated the words in English, then translated.

There was a boy
A very strange enchanted boy
They say he wandered very far, very far
Over land and sea
A little shy and sad of eye
But very wise was he
And then one day
A magic day he passed my way
And while we spoke of many things
Fools and kings
This he said to me
"The greatest thing you'll ever learn
Is just to love and be loved in return"

*

"Ah!" said Keisuke. "Love! What can you be thinking? Love is what kills us!"

But there was gratitude in the look he gave Tomoo. They drank some more, and he said, "Haru gave me your silence, you've given me this song."

And the evening was spent between darkness and light. In the months that followed, Keisuke created a series of magnificent calligraphies and pottery, and Haru organized two exhibitions in Kyōto and Tōkyō that met with great success.

"Despite all the money you take from me, I'm getting rich," said Keisuke. "You are one bastard of an art dealer, but you do a really great job."

Haru had his business life, but he also went on leading his secret life as a father, and before he knew it, Rose had turned nine. Some of the photographs taken with a telephoto lens showed her outside the estate, on foot or on her bike, a breathless, mirthful little explorer, wonderfully alive. One morning, breaking the pact she seemed to have made with herself, Sayoko paused before one of the photographs. It was January, it was snowing, Haru was smoking in his study while reading a report, and he looked up and saw her planted in front of the picture. Rose was laughing wholeheartedly in it, her cap sideways on her head, and she was holding something in her arms. The picture, taken from a distance, did not allow the viewer to see what that thing was. Behind the little girl, in the sun room, a blurry figure was just barely visible.

"It's a kitten," said Sayoko, then after a pause, "And a shadow."

Haru felt a pang of disquiet at her last words, but the months sped by without any other warnings, and then it was Rose's tenth birthday. The weather in France was incredibly fine and warm for October 20—according to the detective—and the photographs showed her in the garden, wearing a coat, sitting before a birthday cake decorated with candles. The photographer had disobeyed Haru's instructions, no doubt inadvertently, for there was one photograph where Maud could be seen sitting on Rose's right, thin and shrunken, but smiling. Haru was so disconcerted by the smile that he didn't get a wink of sleep. That smile reopened prospects it had taken years for him to close. It murmured, What if? It hummed a nagging little melody: And what if? What if? that followed him around all day. He worked, went to the warehouse, made some phone calls, still lulled by that litany. At five o'clock, he took a deep breath and prepared himself to call Manabu Umebayashi in Paris, but just as he was reaching for the receiver, the phone rang. It was Yasujirō, once Ryū Nakamura's right-hand man, now Beth's. All he said was, "You must come to Ichijo." "Now?" asked Haru. "Now," he said.

Haru went out, hailed a cab, and headed toward the Imperial Palace. When the car had left the darkened complex behind, it turned into Ichijo, the street where the Nakamuras lived, and Haru could see flashing lights in the distance. Yasujirō was waiting for him outside the building, his expression so distraught that Haru hardly recognized him. Next to him there were police cars, and an ambulance was pulling away. "Beth?" asked Haru. "William," said Yasujirō. Haru followed him to the apartment, passing policemen as they filed out, their faces somber. The Nakamuras occupied the entire top floor, the big picture windows in the living room overlooking the southern half of the city. In the distance one could see the train station and its mushroom tower, to the left, the temples at the foot of the mountains of the East, to the right, the mountains of the West, bathed in a dark velvet twilight. Beth was sitting on the sofa, and she raised her eyes to him, hard eyes black with pain. She motioned to him to sit down across from her, on another sofa, and Yasujirō left the room, murmuring, "I'll be in the study."

"Talk to me," said Haru, "I don't know what happened."

She raised her hand to say, Wait, and he waited.

"He wanted to leave," she said finally.

She let out a short, horrible laugh.

"Leave?" said Haru.

"He committed suicide."

Haru looked at Beth and, over her shoulder, at the mountains, sparkling with the artificial lights of nighttime. He felt nothing. What was William's Japanese name, he wondered, and a wave of sadness and fear washed over him.

"Stay where you are," she said. "If you come near me, I'll lose it."

She ran her hand across her brow.

"How can we love so much but be so blind?" she said.

She pointed to a sheet of paper in front of her.

"'*I'm leaving*,'" she said. "All he wrote was, 'I'm leaving.'"

She struggled to swallow her saliva.

"There won't be any other explanation. I don't know if I can survive this. I don't even know if I can cry."

"You'll cry later," said Haru, "but for now there's a lot to do. You can count on me."

"That's what I wanted to ask you," she said. "You take care of everything. I'll take care of myself."

He took care of everything. At the funeral, Beth didn't cry, calmly accepting condolences. Forty-nine days later, Haru went with her to the cemetery to place the urn in the Nakamura vault. Next to Ryū's and William's names, she'd had her own engraved, in red characters.

"That's a practice that's disappearing," he said.

"I thought about killing myself, but if I die, who will remember William? And so I've shown my desire to join him, without dying."

"Sorrow is everywhere. We can't get away from it," he said.

"But sometimes, in certain places, with certain people, you'll become another woman, and you'll be able to breathe again."

She looked at him, he saw that his words had done her good, and he said, "Another remarkable woman told me that."

And to himself he added, Another foreign woman.

The next day, Beth went on her own to Nanzen-ji. She paid at the entrance, took off her shoes, put on the temple's horrible leatherette slippers, and walked along the dark gallery to the main garden. It had snowed all night, and the sky was pale. The extreme beauty of the scene thrilled her, as the black-and-white image of snow-covered trees and roofs revealed a different aspect of the place. These pure forms—the sand brushed with white, the bare branches, the powdered slope of roof tiles—spoke of grace and suffering, love and desolation. She felt her body dissolving, her spirit reaching a place—elsewhere—where, for the first time since William's death, she could breathe. The feeling lasted for a long time, then she knelt on the wooden flooring and wept, great life-giving sobs. When she stood up again, emptied, at peace, the pain returned, intact and cruel—But I can come back here as often as I like, she thought, and went away. She called Haru and told him about her morning, and he hung up and reflected on what she had said.

Since her tenth birthday, the photographs had been showing Rose in a different light. She no longer smiled or laughed, and Paule, by her side, looked worried. The photographs arriving from France featured an increasingly sullen little girl, and only the presence of her cat seemed, now and again, to cheer her. Christmas had seemed a sad event: there were no triumphant photos, with presents in hand in the snowy garden, and the first quarterly parcel for 1990 confirmed the ominous implications. Haru looked at the pictures and could not help but think about William. He slept poorly, plagued by nightmares, in anguish on waking. In February, he went to Takayama to visit his family. His father's illness was the same, he was not losing his mind any faster than on Haru's previous visit, something that puzzled the doctors, who had predicted an ongoing deterioration. "We're managing," Naoya would say, whenever Haru questioned him on how the business was doing. That winter was no exception. Haru arrived late in the morning, spent some time at the shop with his brother talking about this and that, then headed for the family home. He found his parents in a rather joyful mood, and, at one point when his father had gone out to fetch some wood, his mother said, "He's taking things more slowly. That's good." For lunch they had a chicken donburi, washed down with warm sake. At the end of the meal, Haru asked what he'd been like at the age of ten, and his father got up, went out of the room, and came back with a square of paper. On the picture, taken over thirty years earlier, Haru was standing on the riverbank behind the house, his upper body half-turned toward the camera. In the background, the torrent could be seen, with frozen pine trees and the huge boulder in its winter cap.

"This was taken on the morning of your tenth birthday," his father said, and he laughed as he added, "You got a bicycle, and you wanted to go into Takayama."

He seemed happy recalling that day. Haru's memory of it was fuzzy. He stared at the yellowed image.

"May I keep it?" he asked, and his mother nodded.

On the road back to Takayama, he marveled at his father's presence of mind—he's here, and he's elsewhere, he thought, he's navigating between both worlds, but we're no better able to communicate than on the day of my tenth birthday. The sun-topped peaks gave Haru the impression they were trying to drive him away. He caught the train to Kyōto and arrived late, took a bath, went to bed, and slept restlessly, troubled by dreams in which a feeling of tenderness and failure prevailed. The instant he awoke, he had a vision of a fox motionless on sparkling ice, then everything returned to nothingness, and he went into the maple room where Sayoko, coming from the kitchen in a cream-colored kimono, brought him his tea. Wordlessly, he handed her the photograph.

"Volcano boy," she said, after looking at it. "The same look."

It was no comfort to him that Rose, however redheaded and French she might be, looked like him. If giving meant understanding, then he neither understood nor gave anything, and, moreover, there was no one he could talk to about Rose and her transformation. For all that she might be a judge and a guide in the way of women, Sayoko was not a confidante; they understood one another but were not in sync, their peculiarities too different for them to talk freely. Although he had never really wondered why, it was impossible for him to confide in Tomoo or Keisuke, and William's death had made it clear to him why he'd always refrained from opening up to Beth. He went on seeing her regularly, but they no longer slept together. The tragedy had distanced them physically, and their friendship, unchanged, had dark overtones he found in other aspects of his life, too, as if something inside him had effected an infinitesimal shift, imperceptibly but surely disrupting the pattern of his days. It was during that time that a Japanese woman just back from ten years abroad with her diplomat husband became his mistress. With her, he discovered a form of lovemaking, tense and feverish, that he'd never known. With the exception of Maud and her cold, dark passivity, sex, for Haru, had always been a light-hearted and amusing game. He loved seduction and giving pleasure, and he thought of it as a sort of miracle no more dramatic than an evening spent drinking sake. Now and again, one of his mistresses would become a friend, and she would speak with a freedom she didn't share with either her husband or often even her own girlfriends, but, even then, he knew how to keep the sex light and charming, with no fear of attachment. Emi was quite the opposite; she'd come into his life and his bed with a hunger that left no room for friendly banter. She wanted him, and pulled him into a spiral of passion kept alive by either the power of her desire or the darkening of his own spirit—he couldn't tell which, but he sensed that the cycle of malediction was driving something he would once have kept at a distance. One evening, when she was across from him in the large tub, naked, offered, intense, he had a burning impulse to tell her about Rose. It was summer, the chirring of cicadas was as shrill as a siren, Emi was looking at him with that mixture of desire and compassion that is so close to love, and he was tempted—By what? he wondered, terrified by the immensity of what he was about to do. She noticed his hesitation and came closer. He studied her lovely mouth and felt so much desire that he entered her there in the water, held her close to him, eager to adhere to her entire body, exhausted, finally, by this desperate embrace. Later, in the bedroom, they lit a cigarette, and she sat with her back against the wall, her legs crossed in front of her.

"Talk to me," she said.

He could not. The following week, they met at an official reception which Haru attended with Keisuke, and Emi with her husband. The reception was held in rooms at the Hotel Okura, and Haru spent his time handing out business cards and networking. After an hour had gone by, Keisuke, mildly tipsy, took refuge in an armchair, where he began to snore discreetly. At one point, he opened his eyes and saw Emi before him, looking at Haru. A few days later, the two men had lunch in a new tonkatsu restaurant on Sanjō, in the shopping arcade.

"What about that woman?" said Keisuke.

"What do you mean?" asked Haru, who knew very well what he meant.

"The possibility of love if, in spite of everything, you agree to accept it."

Haru didn't answer. They finished their breaded pork and their cabbage in yuzu sauce and went out into the arcade. It came to an end thirty yards from there, and beyond it Sanjō-dori, with its concrete and neon lights, extended to the wooded slopes of the mountains of the East. In the glow of summer heat, the urban ugliness seemed even grimier, and the hills, bland and compact, allowed no light to filter through. The forest was sullen, dark and gloomy, streaked with the insults of the modern city's neon. They looked in silence at this blend of old and new Japan, then said goodbye. Haru walked home along the river, passing joggers, walkers, cyclists, and mothers pushing baby carriages. The wild grasses on the riverbanks, scorched by the summer, bowed their plumes toward the water; the river flowed, clear and indifferent. He got home, removed his shoes, went to take a shower, and came to sit, refreshed, at the low table by the maple tree, where Sayoko had left the mail for him. On the little tray, there was only one letter, with a French stamp and his name and address in Latin characters. The handwriting, with high, fine letters, was unfamiliar.

The envelope contained a photograph of Rose in the garden. In the background, white summer lilacs concealed a stone wall. To the right, one could see as far as the Vienne valley. The little girl, in a green smocked dress, was laughing, her nose wrinkled. Haru turned the picture over and read, simply, written in black ink, *Paule*. His heart began to race, and in the hour that followed, he went over the full range of possibilities. How did Paule get his address? It had been on the back of the letter he'd sent to Maud. Did she know he was watching Rose? It was probable, even if maybe this communication was just a message in a bottle. What did she want? He looked at the picture and found nothing to enlighten him, but he felt a tightness in his chest. In the end, Sayoko came in with Mei, the young woman who did the cleaning. He chatted with them until they went into the kitchen, then, looking once again at the photograph, he understood: this was the last photograph from before the dramatic change. Rose was happy in this one, whereas the pictures he'd been receiving lately showed a sad, inscrutable little girl, surrounded by despondency. Paule Arden had sent him the trace of a vanished happiness: her own, her granddaughter's, and—or so she surmised, perhaps—Haru's. He went into his study and questioned his mountains. He felt caught in a vice of malediction. He thought of writing to Paule, but he was afraid that Maud would find out, and when a warm, heavy summer rain began to fall over Kyōto, he told himself once again that the equation of his life could not change. Still, he was moved to discover that halfway round the world there was this elegant woman who knew of his existence and his name, and he took what comfort he could in that salutary thought. Caressed and haunted by Paule's letter, mired in the same impossible situation, the weeks, months, and years went by. His business prospered, there were women in succession, and Rose was growing up, dark and melancholy. Maud was wasting away. He saw his daughter start school at the collège, then the lycée in town, always surrounded by a cordon of smiling schoolmates— But the real dangers are invisible, he thought, and those friends can't protect her like that.

On January 17, 1995, he was asleep in his apartment in Tōkyō when, at 6:30 in the morning, the phone rang. He heard Sayoko say to him, Everything's all right in Kyōto, but Shigeru hasn't heard from his mother—the lines are down. He remembered that her husband's family lived in Kōbe, and he said, How strong was it? They haven't said yet, she replied, but it's serious. He got up and switched on the television. An earthquake measuring 6 with a magnitude of over 7 on the open Richter scale, said the presenter; sadly, it occurred at a shallow depth beneath Awaji Island, and the seismic waves had no time to subside. The first images testified to the destruction of buildings, roads, the Hanshin motorway suspension bridge between Osaka and Kōbe, as well as major fires breaking out all over the area. Like all the Japanese seeing the same images, Haru thought, The survivors are going to be burned to death, and he had trouble breathing. He'd been meant to have dinner with a client in Kōbe just the day before, then sleep at a hotel and take the Shinkansen to Tōkyō first thing in the morning. At the last minute, the client had canceled, the room where he'd planned to put the screen he wanted to buy from Haru had just been flooded—"The tatami are like sponges," he said, laughing down the receiver, "sell me some starfish instead." When Haru managed to get through to him two weeks later, the client told him, "We're alive, but I've lost my house. And you know who was handing out blankets, diapers, water, and instant ramen, just after the earthquake? Not the government, or city hall, or the local administration—they took a week to get their act together. And not any foreign powers, either, since our prime minister so politely declined their offers of aid. It was the yakuza who gave us what we needed to survive the cold. The only ones we could count on were the Japanese people themselves, and the Yamaguchi-gumi."

Haru made a substantial donation to the earthquake victims, and arranged to personally send supplies to people he knew who'd been affected. But the conflagration, for him, wasn't in Kōbe. When his client had canceled that day, he'd decided to go to Tōkyō mid-afternoon, and he'd dined there alone, as he liked to do, in a neighborhood ramen-ya. There, he'd had a long inner dialogue with Rose, made all the more delightful by the ice-cold beer. A few days later, when he saw the images of the devastated area surrounding the hotel in Kōbe where he would have stayed, he felt as if the disaster of Hanshin-Awaji was tearing a new hole in the fabric of his existence. He'd always believed he wasn't afraid of death, and now he realized that wasn't true. To disappear without Rose ever knowing him: this awoke the possibility of his own annihilation. Too little-known as a father, he was becoming a mortal man, and he felt his life grow darker still.

In June 1997, Rose passed the exams for her baccalaureate degree with honors, and Haru went to Meidi-ya, on Sanjō, to buy a bottle of champagne, which he opened that very evening with Keisuke.

"It's disgusting," said Keisuke after taking a first sip. "To what do we owe the honor of putting up with this? Another Frenchwoman in your life?"

Haru didn't answer, and they went back to sake. Rose moved to Paris for university, and he learned that she was studying botany. She lived in her mother's old apartment in the capital, a ten-minute walk from the Gare Montparnasse, the station where the trains left for Touraine. The photographs showed her in various completely new situations, and Haru spent hours going over them. She had friends, admirers, she went out, she partied, but she rarely smiled. One day a photograph captured her at a sidewalk café with a book open before her. In another, she was walking alone in the promenades of the Luxembourg Gardens. The two photographs evoked such sadness that Haru began hating Paris, with its arrogant buildings, symmetrical gardens, and ambience of gilt and wrought iron. Would he like Paris if Rose were happy there? He doubted it, he didn't like the architecture, thought it stank of power and pride. In his daughter, he perceived a harmony of sand and moss imprisoned in an inimical setting. He sensed in her the beating of a Japanese heart, which nothing around her would allow her to hear. He saw her burdened with her mother's angst and with the force of her own blood. She was sullen but hardened against misfortune, inscrutable but unusual, dispossessed of her life yet whole. He wondered whether Maud or he himself would triumph in the end, and so, like the passage of clouds, a decade evaporated, a time marked by extraordinary constancy—business, women, parties, photographs and reports from France—until one morning it was 1999, and a young man by the name of Paul Delvaux arrived in Kyōto.

ELSEWHERE

Haru first met Paul at the home of a client in the northern part of town. Nearby was the Kamigamo shrine, one he loved because it was so close to the wild nature of the northern mountains. He took a stroll there while waiting for his appointment. In the pale winter mist—it was January 18—the torii gates were like monochromatic rainbows. Nearby, the virgin forest of Tadasu lent a primitive, sacred character to the place. He spotted two does at the edge of the trees, and he could tell that snow was on its way. The first flake fell just as he rang Harada-san's doorbell. A young woman came and opened the door and led him into the main room, where he saw the old lady and a young Western man. The two of them were sitting at a low table by the picture window that looked out onto an inner garden, and Haru saw Paul for the first time against a backdrop of bamboo, ferns, and one of the most beautiful stone lanterns he'd ever come across. It was no different from others of the same style—Mizubotaru—but in his opinion, this one was perfectly proportioned. As was the house: old and sublime, with long corridors, wood everywhere, alcoves decorated with magnificent vases, and splendid calligraphies. Harada-san almost never left her house, but the world came gladly to her, this tiny woman, always smiling and extremely rich, with a passion for tea and art. She belonged to a category of clients to whom Haru felt that sales did not really matter. With her, he came to *spend some time*. When she did buy something, he took a smaller margin than usual. He was working for the greater business of art, not business alone, the latter's vanity mitigated by the perfection of the Mizubotaru lantern.

After the customary greetings, Harada-san made the introductions. The young man's name was Paul Delvaux—she had difficulty pronouncing it, so he spelled it out. He came from Belgium, spoke Japanese, and had agreed to be her French teacher. French teacher? said Haru, surprised. A lifelong dream of mine, said the old lady, I don't have much time left to fulfill my dreams, do I? The young woman served them a bowl of matcha and a nerikiri in the shape of a camellia, and Haru placed before Harada-san an object wrapped in pink silk.

"Ah," she said, "I suspect our friend Shibata has something to do with this, am I right?"

They drank their tea in silence, admiring the snowflakes as they fell on the little garden, and Haru noticed that the Western gentleman knew when to keep silent. When Harada-san called for the tea things to be taken away, Haru asked Paul what had brought him to Kyōto. In replying, the young man spoke well, slowly and politely. He and his wife had studied Japanese in Brussels and had received an end-of-studies scholarship at Kyōdai, the most prestigious university in the city. He said this was everything they'd ever dreamed of, to which Harada-san added, "Absolutely, one must dream—and besides, perhaps life itself is nothing but a long dream." Again, silence fell, and she loosened the pink furoshiki. From it she took a box of light wood that had been tied with a flat ribbon trimmed with orange cotton. She untied the ribbon and lifted a white vase out of the box, and Haru could tell, from the signs of an acquaintance of many years, that she was delighted. She told Paul that the vase was to mark the fiftieth anniversary of the day she moved into her house. A priest from Kamigamo would recite a blessing, she would serve tea, and her idea was to put the vase below the calligraphy of a poem by Ryōkan. "But I wanted a contemporary creation," she added. "I needn't give up on what is new simply because I'm old." She smiled briefly, at no one in particular. She was observing the vase. After a moment, she said, "It is truly present," and Haru bowed his head and lowered his eyes. Then he looked up again at Paul, and in his gaze he recognized that particular quality of being both focused and self-oblivious that characterizes decisive encounters. Haru could sense complexity beneath the refined surface, and he liked that mixture of reserve and intensity.

"Are you interested in art?" he asked him.

"I am interested only in art," Paul replied.

"Does it run in the family, perhaps?"

"I come from a line of small Brussels industrialists, Protestant into the bargain, whose taste does not run to the form of things," he said with a laugh. "Austere soup tureens and cheap wine on the table."

They talked about this and that, then Haru complimented him on his excellent Japanese.

"I can't take much credit for that, my best friend in Brussels is from Tōkyō. When I began my studies, he stopped speaking French to me altogether. But my wife speaks Japanese even better than I do."

They turned toward the garden, its bamboo and ferns speckled with fresh snow.

"I came here to spend time with a certain type of art and culture. What you have just put on the table pretty much sums it up."

He looked at the vase.

"Who is the artist?"

"Keisuke Shibata, a potter from Kyōto," Haru replied, "but also a personal friend."

"The entire legacy of a past civilization, seen through the prism of one living man," murmured Paul.

Haru took his leave and walked away in the snow. He went home, inhabited by a curious lightness. When Sayoko brought the tea to his study he said, "I met a very interesting person today. A young man from Belgium."

"Belgium?" said Sayoko, with consternation. "Where did you meet him?"

"At Harada-san's," he replied.

She seemed relieved.

"There is no better place for meeting someone," she said, alluding to the purifying virtues of the forest, or perhaps the powers of the shrine against all the malignant forces of the universe.

So she's given me the green light to meet people from Belgium, thought Haru, then he turned to his business matters and gave Paul Delvaux no further thought. He went out at about four in the afternoon, to meet Beth at a tea house near her home, and as he was going into the building, he came upon the young Belgian, who was just leaving. He was with a young woman, bundled up in an orange coat, who was as petite and dark as he was tall and blonde. Clara, as her husband introduced her to Haru, spoke excellent Japanese, with a fluency and sensitivity that greatly impressed him.

"You love art," he said to Paul. "Come to my house the day after tomorrow for my birthday. I've invited some artist friends, in particular the potter whose vase you saw this morning."

When he saw Paul's look of surprise, Haru added, "I know it's not very common in my country to invite people over. But I'm rather eccentric, as people will tell you."

Later that evening, he recalled with pleasure the young Belgian woman—was it her orange coat, the fact that she was French-speaking, that hint of mischief in her smile? Haru thought about her, and thought about Rose, and a sort of spell came over him. At around midnight, he went out to meet Keisuke at a bar in the city center and found him in the company of a few regulars, and of Jacques Melland, whom he greeted with delight. He asked for news of his son. "Édouard's in Shanghai," said Melland. "He's very good at negotiating with the Chinese; that's one less job for me to see to." Haru thought Melland didn't look very well, and after they'd exchanged some more of their news, Melland said something which, in the ambient hubbub, Haru did not catch, but from Melland's eyes, he understood. Other guests arrived, chairs were moved around, Melland began a discussion with Tomoo, and Keisuke came and collapsed on the chair next to Haru. Haru told him that Harada-san had liked the vase, and he thought she would buy it. The potter laughed.

"So she can stick it under some tacky pretty poem," he said.

But when Haru was headed back to Kamo-gawa, caught in a whirl of disorderly little snowflakes, he thought again of Ryōkan's verses, of Clara Delvaux, of Rose, and of the garden at the house in Kamigamo with a feeling of potent renewal. He took a bath, read for a while, and lapsed into a peaceful sleep.

the garden in tranquility
as the camellia
gives its white light

Haru had white camellias delivered for his birthday. Sayoko, as focused as an athlete, arranged them in a tall, dark vase. At seven in the evening, a crowd of friends arrived, Keisuke in the lead, then reinforcements came over the course of the evening. When Beth made her entrance, Keisuke bowed deeply.

"The Iron Lady," he said. "How many poor wretches has your empire exploited this week?"

"At least I don't put any pretty little poems above your masterpieces," she said.

"You're such a traitor," said Keisuke to Haru.

Not long afterward, the Delvaux arrived, and Clara made the same refreshing impression on Haru as two days earlier. She was wearing a pale pink dress, simple but elegant, and he thought of Rose, and the does at Tadasu. Paul stood smiling next to her, tall, fair-haired, and reserved. Haru introduced them to a few guests, and the evening continued. Friends who were musicians played the koto and the shamisen, and Sayoko dispatched French-style canapés from the kitchen. Keisuke sniffed them suspiciously. "But the chef is Japanese," Beth said. "You should get off your island someday." "The entire world is an island," he retorted, wolfing down a tiny piece of toast with teriyaki foie gras. In its glass cage, the maple tree bowed low with its burden of snow. Haru went from one group to the next, but he realized that his gaze regularly returned to Clara and Paul—I'm glad they're here, he thought, studying the young woman as she laughed and spoke to Tomoo. At around ten o'clock, Keisuke, already completely plastered, started singing a traditional New Year's song, changing the poetic words for ribald ones, and Haru saw Paul laugh and drink a great deal without ever getting drunk.

At eleven o'clock, Jacques Melland rang at the door of the house by the Kamo-gawa, and Sayoko, who was on her way out, let him in. She raised a hand to her heart. "You can't intimidate me anymore," said Jacques Melland to her, in French. "You're an ally, I know that now." She went on her way. Haru walked over to Melland when he saw him, and they sat alone in a corner of the room, speaking English.

"Two days ago at the bar, I could tell you didn't really hear what I said," Melland explained, "so I'll say it again, here where it's quiet: this will probably be my last trip to Kyōto."

"I'm not surprised," said Haru. "I can see how tired you are."

"If only it were just fatigue," said Melland. "Whatever the case may be, I wanted to see you to tell you something you already know, but at death's door, we have our unexpected little whims. I don't know why it's made me so talkative, I've always hated any sort of sentimentality."

"You love art, and you love your son," said Haru. "There's nothing sentimental about that."

"I don't even know what I love," said Jacques Melland, "but who cares now? Anyway, that is what I wanted to tell you: my life had only one hour of fervor to give, and I've known that hour, thanks to you."

"At Shinnyo-dō," said Haru.

"At Shinnyo-dō," said Melland, "protected by a sky where gardens were withering. It's astonishing that a place can be endowed with such power, but I felt a profound joy there, the joy of being wholly in phase with myself. And do you know the best thing about this story? I've always thought of myself as a dissatisfied man who would die ruminating on his regrets. But now that the time has come for me to leave this world, I'm filled with wonder to think that I really did experience that hour."

He emptied his cup of sake in one go.

"Don't get me wrong: it's not a memory I recall with joy, something that might've helped me live through all the other hours. It's become part of my flesh, my bones, my blood; it has become an integral part of me. I am that brief, furious fervor."

He looked puzzled.

"I know that must sound insane."

"Not at all," said Haru. "It's all I dare hope for, for myself, when the day comes."

Melland tapped on the table with his index finger.

"Before I bid farewell, I have a favor to ask you."

"I'm at your service," said Haru.

"I'd like you to keep an eye on Édouard. Take him in, guide him. He can learn so much from a man like you. He's not very well-balanced, but he does have substance, you'll see."

"Of course," said Haru. "You can count on me."

Melland leaned back against the sofa, like a man relaxing after a long day. Time is nothing, thought Haru, the only moments that endure are the remarkable ones, everything else vanishes, and here we are, gazing at the pillars emerging from the fog.

"Do you still have my little sculpture?" asked Jacques, referring to the cast of the primitive goddess he'd given Haru twenty years earlier to thank him for the lines from Rilke.

"Of course I do," said Haru. "It's a cast from the Louvre, isn't it?"

"The original, which they found at Lespugue, in Haute-Garonne, is over twenty thousand years old," said Jacques, "and it looks like some of your *dogū* statues. I know you're not really interested in Western art, but these works are the primeval root of art, they have no nationality, they don't belong to any given territory. Everything branched out after that, and everyone likes to see their own progeny in it, but this proof that it all came from the same original womb, from the universal desire to give form to matter, is something I've always found moving."

He gave a disillusioned little laugh.

"Unlike you, I don't much care for my own culture; I'm completely devoted to yours."

"I lack imagination or audacity," Haru replied. "I admire the way you can appreciate something that's not familiar to you."

The Frenchman went on to mingle with the guests, drank a great deal and laughed just as much, poked a camellia into his buttonhole, and took his leave soon after midnight, waving his hand as if he'd be back the next day. Haru followed him with his gaze, then, turning to Paul, he thought suddenly, I may be Japanese, but I seek out what's foreign—or maybe it's the other way around, I only tear myself away from who I am so that I can constantly return to myself; I'm fated to go around and around the same loop, relentlessly. He went to sit next to Paul and Keisuke, who were chatting, propped against the maple tree cage.

"Belgians are not as dumb as I thought," Keisuke said, pointing at Paul. "He's a good talker, a good drinker, and he has a good eye—all that and he's only twenty-two."

Across from Haru, the camellias' exquisite whiteness mingled with the wave of sadness and sweetness that flowed through him.

"What have you been talking about?" he asked Paul.

"About his vase," the young man replied. "I didn't know you could be modern and ancient at the same time. You can only really grasp it in the presence of a true work of art."

Keisuke mumbled something, tilted his head to one side, and began snoring.

"You are everything I would like to become," Paul said to Haru.

He said it calmly, without gushing, but Haru had already made up his mind.

"Then come and work for me," he said.

T wo months later, Haru received a letter from Édouard Melland. My father has died, he wrote, but just before he passed away, he asked me to tell you something, and I'm re-transcribing it here just the way he put it: I understand the fox. Haru mused about this return of the Heian tale among the themes in his life, at a time when Paul and Clara's presence had given it a new direction. In reality, whenever he had combined sincerity and calculation in his career, the equation had proven successful. He liked Paul, Paul was Belgian and Protestant, he spoke Japanese, he loved art, he knew how to drink and when to be silent: it should be possible to make an art dealer out of him. To top it all, he was young, and Haru sensed that he was clever without being inauthentic. In every respect, therefore, it seemed a reasonable wager.

"What do I need to know?" Paul had asked on the evening of Haru's birthday party.

"Three things," Haru replied. "Nurture silence. Never rush anything."

He stopped speaking. Paul waited, then smiled. "And be on time, I suppose."

Haru took him everywhere, introducing him as his assistant. When people nonchalantly asked him why he had chosen a Belgian, he smiled and said, "It's a small country." They nodded, not really understanding, but Haru could see that his answer inspired trust. If he sensed any resistance, he would add, "A little European island," and he won them over. In fact, Belgium brought an exotic touch to his business at a time when he felt that if he were to have lasting success, he must try new things. Paul Delvaux spoke slowly, learned quickly, and took a visible pleasure in salesmanship. He observed, never interrupted, learned to smile, to bow, and to lower his eyes, all at the proper rhythm. The Japanese, once they got over their initial surprise, appreciated his discretion and concluded that what they'd found incongruous at first was actually very chic. To come across a Westerner who was so quiet and didn't talk about himself was a positive anomaly that canceled out the potentially negative impact of his origins. And Paul continued to remain silent and drink with tact.

But when the two of them were alone together at the warehouse or at Haru's place by the Kamo-gawa, they did talk. They talked about the artwork, the clients, they talked figures and markets, and then they would talk about something quite different, art itself, and life, and—with surprising ease—themselves. To this practice that Haru already shared with Keisuke and Tomoo, Paul brought a window onto a new world, something Haru found refreshing. It didn't take the form of secrets or monologues, their exchanges were spontaneous and desultory, and for each of them these moments were a gift each man gave as generously to the other as to himself. Moreover, they were aware that this was only possible because they were foreigners to each other, and that this mutual foreignness negated the hierarchical relationship that would otherwise exist due to age and position. At work, they used the appropriate pronouns and hid the fact that in private they were much less formal. On October 20, 1999, the day of Rose's twentieth birthday, Haru took Paul into his study. The young man initially saw only the view out onto the river and the mountains, and then, turning back, he saw the photographs on the cypress wood panels. He went closer and examined them in silence. Haru lit a cigarette and poured some sake, then Paul went to sit across from him, and they drank, still in silence.

"Your daughter," said Paul, finally.

"Today is her twentieth birthday," said Haru.

"No one knows?" asked Paul.

"Only Sayoko."

"Apart from her?"

"No one."

He told him everything: Maud, her proscription, the private detective, the photographer, Paule, the dramatic change, the cats and shadows. He told him about the ten days he had spent with the Frenchwoman; he talked about Emmanuelle Revers and repeated her last words to him. He described his pride as a father, his sorrow as a father, the cross he bore and the hope he nurtured as a father, his terror after William's suicide and the earthquake in Kōbe.

"Now I understand better why Beth is such a hard woman," said Paul.

Haru felt exhausted, but a strange euphoria was coming over him.

"I've been waiting years for this," he said. "Can you carry this burden?"

"Burden?" Paul said. He laughed. "This is a gift."

And thus began a happy period. What Haru had not been able to do with Emmanuelle Revers had become possible with a man, because Paul, too, in Clara's footsteps, was guided by the way of women. Whenever they met, Haru felt his fondness for the young Belgian woman grow a little stronger. Her disposition was, by turns, joyful, refined but simple, and funny, with an exquisite touch of mischief. She made Paul's life easy and luminous; she appreciated the life of the mind, managed everyday matters pragmatically, and, something Haru found lovelier still, took care of everything without wanting to control anything. Not long after he had revealed Rose's existence to Paul, he said to him, "You can tell Clara," to which Paul replied that he had no secrets from his wife except other people's, and with a laugh he added, "And yet she claims I'm the most secretive person she knows." Which he was. He didn't hide anything, but he was inhabited by such impenetrable complexity that it concealed entire facets of his inner life from himself, and from others as well. He talked not only about his family, around whom he felt stifled, or his Japanese studies, which he had undertaken to follow Clara, or his arrival in Japan, where he had immediately felt at home, but he also shared his likes, his thoughts, his doubts, his questioning. Finally, every three months they would go over the reports and photographs from France together, and Paul's input turned up things that Haru had missed altogether. Now, in addition to Sayoko's *kami* and *yōkai* and his own intuition, came this Western wisdom, building a bridge between Maud's depression and the language of mountain foxes.

Almost two years after they first met, Haru took Paul to Takayama. It was October, Rose would soon be twenty-one, the weather was fine, and the car sped between mountain slopes glowing red and their immaculate white peaks. His parents and brother had gone to a funeral, the house on the bank of the stream was deserted, and, in the middle of the torrent, the great boulder with its autumn crown of moss seemed to divide the turbulent current in two. Haru told Paul how he'd grown up watching the snow fall and melt on that boulder, and how rocks, trees, waterfalls, and ice had shaped his entire vocation. They gazed out at the rushing water. Paul knelt down and placed the palm of his hand on the earth of the riverbank, where carmine red maple leaves had fallen.

"Form is the beauty of the surface," he said, standing back up. "No doubt that's what I like so much about Japan. It has rescued me from my depths."

In the train headed home, while Paul was sleeping, Haru thought about what he'd said, and other words came back to him unexpectedly: *Sadly, the quake occurred at a shallow depth, and the seismic waves had no time to subside.* That's exactly it, he thought, that's the Japanese soul, exactly: through our land and our destiny, we're condemned to stay close to the surface, and, cut off from our inner depths, we're struck full on by disasters and cataclysms. Then, once the desolation has been sown, we transform the nightmare into something beautiful, and we look deep into the withering heavens. At that moment, he thought about his father and concluded, Healthy or sick, we've never been close; we've stayed near the surface, and everything in my life has been sculpted by that impossible depth.

P aul never commented on Haru's decisions. When it came to work, and to Rose, he listened, and sometimes asked a question at the end. As a businessman, he'd grasped everything—the manner, the style, the obstacles and tricks. He was exceptional. One evening, they were at a bar with Tomoo and Keisuke, and Keisuke said, looking first at Paul, then at Haru: "The same model."

When the young man raised a questioning eyebrow, Keisuke added, "You're a bastard, just like him, even if your style is more tactful, less brutal, and what's more, you're Belgian—we can't tell what you've got up your sleeve. If you'd been French, you'd have been less of a mystery; the French are so predictable. But like him, you'll squeeze art like a lemon, then toss it into the grave of your disappointed ambitions."

"What ambitions?" asked Paul.

"I'm asking you," said Keisuke, "but fortunately your wife has saved you."

"And what about me," said Haru. "Who'll save me?"

"Something has saved you," said Keisuke, "but you're hiding it from me."

When they were alone, Paul asked Haru why he'd never told Keisuke about Rose.

"He's lost two children," Haru replied. "How could I tell him about my failures as a father?"

"He's a friend."

"We have different relationships with each of our friends,"

said Haru. "Don't ask me to explain it. Explanation is a Western disease."

They celebrated the turn of the millennium at Shinnyo-dō. All of Kyōto was there, including Beth, who didn't like festivity. That evening, Tomoo introduced Akira to them, a former *butō* dancer who was his age—in his sixties—and who'd just moved into the sailing ship. Fifteen years had gone by since Isao's death, and Keisuke placed a brotherly hand on his old friend's shoulder. Akira, who had once been a truly great dancer, looked like a gentle, smiling, little old man, but when he stood up to perform a parody of kabuki, everyone could feel the power emanating from that body long accustomed to exploring the shadows. The parody itself was hilarious, and Haru enjoyed seeing Clara and Paul roar with laughter. There was other entertainment—piano, songs both traditional and bawdy—and then at around midnight, a shakuhachi player came to balance out the duel between gaiety and gravity, that trademark of the sailing ship, by releasing from his instrument a flow of trembling, melancholy notes onto the gathering. As the more casual acquaintances gradually began to leave, the party settled into a fog of sake and friendship, and Haru, sitting with his back against a partition, allowed himself to drift. They talked and drank and toasted Clara and Paul's purchase of a little house near Kamigamo. "So," said Beth, "you're settling in among us for good?" "Paul is working for Haru, I'm filling in at the university's French department; it's all beyond our wildest dreams," Clara replied, adding, "Seen from this vantage point, Belgium is more dreary than ever." "And yet, it's a small country," said Paul, and as they were all familiar with Haru's tricks, they laughed wholeheartedly. Beth and Clara left at four in the morning, Akira went to bed, and the only ones left drinking were Paul, Tomoo, Keisuke, and Haru—the final foursome, thought Haru, in the end everything always comes down to one last quartet, to keep the shadows away. When the others had fallen asleep on the tatami, he walked back to the house by the Kamo-gawa with Paul. There, they went on drinking and talking, until the young man got up and went to examine the wooden panel with the latest photographs from France. Rose, now an agricultural engineer, was in Paris doing research in botanical geography. Over the years she had stayed just the same: sharp and austere, somber and constantly angry. She had many lovers whom she dismissed diligently. Haru thought she was beautiful and unusual, wholly herself and in despair, but he saw that the anger in her was gradually yielding to indifference. As day was breaking, he confided in Paul, who reflected a moment, then eventually said, "There's more sadness in her now." The night was ending, the maple quivered slightly, the lingering echo of the notes from the shakuhachi enveloped it in invisible silk, soft and deep. Once Paul had left, Haru gazed out at his river, above which tiny snowflakes were dancing. Everything in his life seemed immobile; seasons passed, and Kyōto changed and stayed the same, as ageless and new as rushing water. The Delvaux had broken the cycle of malediction, but nothing, no one, seemed able to break the cycle of prohibition. Haru was getting ready to take a bath when Sayoko appeared suddenly, wearing a kimono printed with snow-covered mountains, and her face was unusually animated. She placed a little tray with fresh mochis on the low table in the maple room, went to prepare the tea, then came to sit across from Haru.

"Her name is Sora," she said. "She was born in the first minute of January 1 of the year 2000."

"You're a grandmother now," Haru said, congratulating her. "I'm very happy for you."

They drank their tea in silence, in the close understanding of two people who've known each other for two decades. A newborn baby—born in the New Year, could there be any better omen, Haru mused, and, suddenly, he realized that his daughter might have children someday, and he was overcome by a dizziness that made him briefly forget Sayoko. "I beg your pardon?" he said, when he realized she was talking to him.

"Wouldn't you like to have a driver?" she was saying.

"A driver?" he echoed, failing to understand.

"A driver," she repeated, and he knew it would be futile to resist.

The following day, she introduced the driver to Haru. She had approached him for the job on her own. Masa Kanto, whom everyone called Kanto, was the late-born son of her third sister. They all thought there was something slightly wrong with him—"He's just a little bit autistic," Paul would say—but he was good with computers, and he worked at home, in Tōkyō, whenever he was contracted for a job, at a pace that suited him. Sayoko had found him a little apartment with a garage, near Hyakumanben, five minutes from the house by the Kamo-gawa. All Haru had to do was call, and Kanto would come, then go back to his computers once he'd finished driving. To be honest, Haru rather liked the idea of no longer having to resort to those overheated taxis, with their hackneyed conversations and their smell of old bento, and Kanto would prove to be a good driver who knew how to keep quiet and how to converse, who was always pleased with his lot in life. He liked the absence of schedule, he liked the work—"Otherwise I'd be at home all day eating junk from the *konbini*," he said. What was more, he loved Kyōto, and gradually Haru took him to the temples, the gardens, the cafés, and, occasionally, to a restaurant. One day he asked him what he liked about the Silver Pavilion, and Kanto replied, "The ponds." "Why?" said Haru. "They are *precise*," Kanto replied, and Keisuke, who was in the car, laughed and said, "That's what I missed in my latest ink drawing." As for Haru, he felt distracted, sensing that something had changed. Time was transformed by his sudden understanding that lineages continued into the future in the same way he'd seen them perpetuated through his ancestors' past. He observed Kanto, listened when Sayoko talked to him about her granddaughter, and he thought, I'm swimming in an invisible, ever-flowing current, and my daughter is there, too, each of us for all eternity in a precise position it is pointless to hope to change.

Every year, the last descendant of another lineage, Édouard Melland, came for an extended stay at the end of spring and the end of autumn. His Japanese was proficient now, and he said he only managed to get through the other months of the year thanks to the prospect of this time he would spend in Kyōto. One day when he was at Haru's place, and Beth was there, he explained that his trips to China were the hell that justified Kyōto, and Haru saw that she was looking at him attentively. A little later, the Frenchman told them that, nine years ago, his father had asked to have white camellias placed in his coffin. "I don't know why I didn't tell you this then," he said to Haru, "but I was obsessed with my mission of passing on his words about the fox." After a pause: "Then I was afraid to bring it up again." In reply, Haru told him the story of the fox and the lady from Heian—"This story is very powerful, but I don't know why," he added, and thinking about Emmanuelle Revers, "The friend who held the key to it has also passed away." Édouard went back home again, and Haru was left with the sensation that something, somewhere, had *mutated*. Then he gave it no more thought and went out to dinner with Tomoo, Akira, and Paul at Kitsune, a yakitori-ya that had recently opened a stone's throw from the sailing ship. The monsoon was drawing near, the air was cool, a slight drizzle draped the mountains of the East in gray. The yakitori-ya, run by a former Kyōdai student, welcomed students and locals who didn't know Haru and didn't care whether they knew him or not. The place was like a childhood attic where, amid the manga posters, rusted metal signs, and figurines of superheroes, rows of sake bottles stood as a rampart against the smoke from the grill. The walls were painted black, and a few hanging lamps cast a dim light over the room with its dark wooden tables, its beer crates in the stairway, the rotary dial phone on the counter. Above all, they served flavorful, tender skewers of meat and, according to Keisuke, the best chicken salad in town. Paul had told them he'd be late, so Haru, Tomoo, and Akira ordered ice cold beer and edamame while they waited. In the cool, uncertain, mysterious atmosphere of pre-monsoon days, the early evening was proving a delight to Haru, until at around eight o'clock Sayoko called him with some housekeeping query, and just before she hung up she said, "There's a strange atmosphere this evening." As always, he thought about France and Rose, but then Paul showed up, ordered a bottle of sake, and said, "I have some news." And once the sake had been poured: "Clara is expecting—our little girl is due in January." "How do you know it's a girl?" asked Tomoo. "I just do, that's all," Paul replied, and he looked at Haru. From one father to another, thought Haru, and, finding himself perched precariously on a narrow ridge between joy and sorrow, he raised his cup and said, "I envy that little girl for having the best parents on earth." A profound well-being came over him. He was happy for Paul and relieved that Sayoko's premonition was not about Rose. He saw the future opening wide, was moved to be a witness and a friend, was curious about the child to come, and was as sure as Paul that it would be a girl. Oddly enough, to know this little foreigner would be arriving in Kyōto before too long dispelled the apprehension he'd been feeling about the fate of his own child in Paris. He went back to the house by the Kamo-gawa, took a bath, and fell asleep, lulled by a sense of both plenitude and excitement. The following morning he came upon Sayoko in the maple tree room, with the long face she wore on bad days.

"Clara is pregnant," he said.

She frowned. "Will it be a girl?" she asked.

He nodded. She sniffed.

"What's wrong?" he asked.

"I don't know."

He worked all morning in his study, still buoyed up by the feeling of plenitude from the previous night, and when Paul called him before leaving for Tōkyō, he said again, "I'm so happy for you." "Clara, too," Paul replied with a laugh, "she's happy for both of us, even though she has to do all the work." It was June 20, it was chilly; Haru hung up, and the skies opened in a torrential downpour. He shivered, his mood changed, and he thought again about what Édouard had said the previous day about the white camellias in his father's coffin. He pictured Jacques Melland, pale and motionless, an ascot around his neck, bouquets of fresh flowers on his chest, in the peace of the ultimate whiteness. He was a traveler, thought Haru, he came to the ends of the earth looking for the material for his final dwelling-place—but I have never left my archipelago, even though my heart's purpose is, similarly, on the far side of the night. Tired of his own mood swings, he was about to get up, but Sayoko, looking worried, came into the room, and just then his cell phone rang. He took the call in her presence and heard Akira say, "Tomoo just died."

All of Tomoo's close friends came to the wake. It was not very common anymore, to have a wake at home, but they did, all the same, at the sailing ship of Shinnyo-dō, and Hiroshi, Keisuke's brother, officiated. Tomoo's parents and sister had already passed away, and there were not many family members at the ceremony. Haru sat at the piano, next to his friend's body. He was crushed, heavy with sorrow and solitude, and Keisuke summed it all up when he murmured, "And in the nights the heavy earth falls from among the stars toward solitude." In the terrible calm of the room, Haru, seated below the photograph of Kazuo Ōno, could not imagine drinking and talking the way they had at Isao's wake. He said to himself, We think we're stronger, but death inhabits us. Outside, a heavy rain was falling. He was in pain but couldn't weep. He was probing his shadows.

Half the city came to the funeral, and they all paid their respects to Akira. At the end, he began to speak, thanking everyone for being there and adding a few words in the glacial silence of the funeral home: "He didn't suffer, he didn't know he was dying. He passed away in the armchair where his first great love had died. I was the second. There will be no others." Many people from the national television station were there; they'd come all the way from Tōkyō, Osaka, and even Sapporo, all places where, in keeping with the NHK's principle of rotating postings, Tomoo had worked in succession, keeping the sailing ship as his base. About the ship, Keisuke suddenly said, "We can't go to Shinnyo-dō anymore, without our Tochan." They agreed to meet at Haru's place. They got horribly drunk, were incapable of speaking or laughing, and fell asleep wherever they happened to be in the room. Alone among them, Paul left during the night, and Haru went to take a solitary bath. In the water, he was overwhelmed with sorrow, and with it came a new realization—Tomoo didn't know he was dying, and we didn't know we've all been getting older, and before long my daughter's father will be an old man. Sae, Yōko, Ryū, Tarō, William, and Isao had all died young, but his old parents in Takayama were still alive. Jacques Melland, who'd been ten years older, could have been seen as a first warning sign, but he was a foreigner, and was far away from Haru's everyday life when he took his final leave. Tomoo's death, however, brought a radical transformation to that everyday life: it changed the number of friends, the equilibrium between venues, the texture of time, and, like never before in his life, Haru began to think about his age.

They met up again at Shinnyo-dō the following week to bury their friend's ashes. "He would have hated for me to dine alone talking to an urn," Akira told Keisuke, to justify not respecting the customary forty-nine days. In return, Keisuke said, "You have to act quickly with corpses so that all you have to contemplate is death." On the morning of June 28, Akira, Keisuke, and Haru headed to the cemetery. Tochan's deserted house had something of a mausoleum about it, so they didn't linger. Haru knew he would not go back there again. It was drizzling, and the heartbreak of having to bid farewell to thirty years of a life of friendship was heavy with trembling raindrops. The men made their way along a cold, muddy path of desolation, mournful with memories. They stood by the tomb in silence, feeling empty and stupid, then they went in the direction of

Kurodani and came to the top of the great stairway. Below them was the city, like a flow of concrete lava between the hills, rumbling with indifference. While they gazed dolefully out at it, Keisuke said, "This time, the sake won't save us, but Kyōto will," and they felt the city's healing power spread through them. The following week, Haru came back with Paul on his regular walk along the Shinnyo-dō loop. At the foot of the steps, he paused at the spot where Melland had apprised him of Rose's existence, and he thought about how his own ashes would be buried there, and how it would connect his fate to Tomoo's, making their tombs neighbors and their deaths complicit. He felt calmer. They had dinner at the yakitori-ya where they'd had their last meal all together, and he came away with the certainty that Kitsune, a protected enclave of childhood, would preserve his happy moments.

The next day at dawn, Naoya called and informed Haru that their father—like Tomoo—had died in his sleep. Haru took the first train to Takayama, rented a car at the station, went to drop his things off at Kakurezato, and joined his family at the funeral home. An impressive crowd turned out for the funeral: fellow brewers, tradesmen, and friends, but also men and women Haru did not know. They all greeted him in a way that made him feel both like a native of the town and a man who had done well, and he knew that he was admired and, at the same time, excluded from this gathering of goodwill. His mother brought with her the self-effacement and melancholy he'd always known her to have, and which grief had only reinforced. At one point during the ceremony, she wept soundlessly, her shoulders shaking. Naoya's wife placed a hand on her arm, and she went on crying in silence. A memory came to Haru from his stay in the mountains when he had first learned of his father's illness. In Haru's darkened mind, the taste of mushrooms was tinged with obscurity and trembling, but just as he wanted to leave this scene haunted by ghosts, the stars, guiding him along the way of his ancestors, had held him back. Now, a father himself and perhaps, someday, a grandfather, he imagined the ancestor he, too, would become, and he saw his life inscribed in the entirety of time, where the same scene was repeated relentlessly—between his parents and himself, between himself and his daughter, and, quite soon perhaps, between his daughter and her own children—the same scene of silence and solitude.

He stayed at Kakurezato for three days, devoting time to his mother, seeing his cousins and old friends, talking about brewing with Naoya, and walking in the mountains while thinking about Tomoo. On the morning of the fourth day, he headed back to the train station, winding his way along the valley between the flooded rice fields, the modest homes, warehouses, and little rain-drenched shrines. The abundant vegetation, the luxuriant vegetable gardens, the white stones revealed by the low water of early summer brought warm whiffs of childhood innocence to his journey. He took his foot off the gas pedal and slackened the speed, until at last he found peace. He went past the family shrine, rolled down the window, and let the warm, humid air caress his face as he yielded to the welcome of his mountains. He drove for a while through the familiarity of things, then something changed, and he felt he was *elsewhere*. The usual scenery faded, as if inserted into the wider setting, intangible but present, of a new world. In this landscape without horizons, he withdrew into himself, where he found a vast territory and thought, So, elsewhere is here.

On January 10, 2009, ten days before Haru's sixtieth birthday, Paul and Clara's daughter was born. Haru went to the maternity clinic to meet the infant, whom they'd named Anna Rose Yōko: "Rose for my grandmother, Yōko for Keisuke, and Anna for a life out of a novel," Clara explained. Paul said nothing, but smiled. Haru was fascinated by the power of life that emanated from the newborn baby. Halfway around the world, his own daughter was full of life, and it was with intense power and sorrow that he felt her resonance. A few days later, Beth came to Kamigamo, her arms full of lovely presents. In the vestibule, she shook Paul's hand and said, with sincere affection, "Clara and Anna have sentenced you to happiness." On the evening of his sixtieth birthday, Haru hosted a huge reception, primarily focused on the running of his business, and Paul, with dark circles under his eyes, played his part to perfection. From the start, it was obvious that Anna would be dark and slender like her mother, and Paul pointed out to Haru that they had both fathered daughters who didn't look anything like them. Sayoko was besotted with the little girl; she laughed with her whenever her father brought her to the house by the Kamo-gawa, but continued to watch over her in her stubborn, vigilant way. Nevertheless, the year went by uneventfully, and in early 2010, a relieved Haru thought that they'd made it through, unscathed. On Sunday, January 10, Paul stopped by in haste to drop off some papers before taking his family to Kokedera for Anna's first birthday. When he came back, he said, "It's the season of mists; it's sublime," and Haru set aside a time the following week when he, too, could go there. He hadn't been to the moss temple in ages, and on the morning of January 17, Kanto drove him to Arashiyama, in the western part of the city. On the way, they chatted, and Haru was surprised and amused to learn that Kanto enjoyed Noh plays.

"I thought your young, high-tech generation wasn't interested in Noh plays," he said. "It's mostly older people like me who go to see them."

"I'd like very much to go to the Takigi-Noh festival in June," said Kanto.

This was an annual outdoor festival, held in the immense courtyard of the Heian Shrine, where two of the city's Noh companies performed. At nightfall, great torches were lit. Haru had never been, either.

"What is it you like about Noh?" he asked.

"The truth," said Kanto.

They reached the entrance to Kokedera just in time. The gate was opened on the hour to the waiting visitors, a handful of retired people armed with huge cameras. Haru greeted them politely. Everyone followed the monk to a large hall where they were asked to sit on the tatami for the customary ritual of the heart sutra—chant and writing. Then thin strips of wood were handed out, on which they were asked to write a wish. Haru, who hadn't come for that, stuffed the strip into his pocket, wondering what Rose would make of this ritual that, ordinarily, he appreciated, and the embryo of an idea began to germinate in his mind. Just then, they were told they could spend the rest of the visit on their own, outside. They were shown the way to the far end of the inner enclosure, and from there, at last, they would be free to explore the woods next to the temple. On the ground, a thick, velvety, almost phosphorescent moss covered the roots and stones. Farther along was a clearing where thin bands of winter mist were rising from a pond. All around, the black branches of January scripted a secret poem. Haru went into the woods and strolled through shards of pale sunlight. He paused, looked up at the cypress trees, the bare branches of the maples. They're motionless, he thought, but they give life; meanwhile, we tear up our roots to flee from our own shadows. Then, recalling similar thoughts he'd had when leaving his mountains after his father's death: Elsewhere is here, in transformation.

He came to the end of his walk and went out, regretfully. The earth of Kokedera assuaged grief, purified love, dusted the web of life with a sparkling powder—it's a magical land, he mused, a land of metamorphosis. He thought of Anna and Rose, and began picturing how they would meet one day, and, for the first time in a very long time, he felt profoundly happy.

T he next day, he told Paul about his visit and his hopes. "When we were there, Anna couldn't stop laughing," Paul said. "Our girls will go there together when we're so old we can't walk." They spent the rest of the morning working. At around noon, while they were having coffee by the maple tree cage, Paul had a call from Clara. He hung up, a worried look on his face. "What's the matter?" asked Haru. "I don't know, but something's wrong," said Paul. "Anna?" asked Haru. "No," he said, and went out. Haru, uneasy, lit a cigarette, and the afternoon went by in troubling uncertainty. Sayoko had taken her day off, and he was sorry not to have her there, his malediction compass. At eight o'clock that evening, Paul called him. "Clara has cancer," he said. "We don't know anything more for the moment. She'll have more tests later this week." "I'm here," Haru assured him. A few days later, Paul said, "It's a pregnancy-related cancer that affects young women with small children. It's very aggressive." "I'm here," Haru said again, but he knew his friends were alone. He used his connections to find the best doctors and the best care, but he was helpless to break open the solitude in which the illness had confined Paul and Clara. The first months of treatment were very trying for the young woman: Sayoko, bitter prophetess, turned into a good fairy, looking after Anna, Paul went on working, and Haru, aware that the cruelty of malediction would dictate its natural calendar, did not suggest that he take time off. To celebrate Anna's second birthday, Beth and Keisuke joined Haru and Paul in the room where Clara, thin and exhausted, lay on her bed, smiling at everyone. At the end of February, Paul told Haru there was little hope, and Laura, Clara's sister, came from Belgium to stay with them. In the evening, once his wife and daughter were asleep, Paul left Laura in charge and went to the house by the Kamo-gawa. He came into the little garden, propped his bicycle against the wall, and joined Haru in his study. There they drank sake and conversed in the dark. On the threshold of disaster, the things that separated human beings were erased, and Haru wondered if he'd ever been this close to anyone. Paul was not the only one talking; it was a shared dialogue. They listened to each other, spoke about their lives, worried about Clara and Anna and, after a certain point in time, about the little girl's future without her mother. Paul didn't complain, didn't evade anything—"If it weren't for Anna, I'd kill myself once Clara's gone," he said one evening, and another time, "She's in too much pain. It can't go on." When Haru relayed this to Beth, she gave a short, dry laugh that pained them both. Early in the afternoon of March 10, Sayoko, busy arranging a plum tree branch in a vase, stopped suddenly and sniffed the air, looking puzzled. Two hours later, Clara was briefly hospitalized, but Sayoko didn't seem alarmed. It's not that, thought Haru, or in any case, not yet.

On the morning of March 11, 2011, Haru met with a client at home before going out to have lunch with Akira. They drank beer and talked about Tomoo with a shared affection—"At our age, we're orphans," they said, laughing. Akira added, "If you only knew how much I loved him," and Haru thought of Isao, of these men who had a talent for love, his nostalgia and melancholy colored with tenderness. At around two o'clock, he went alone to Shinnyo-dō and set off on his weekly loop, but at the top of the great Kurodani steps, he was stricken with a sudden headache. He went down the steps to the place where he'd learned of

Rose's existence, and the migraine became so intense that he was forced to crouch down. After a few minutes, he stood back up and finished his walk, met Kanto outside the great red gate, and asked to be dropped off at the warehouse where, in response to a strange premonition, he switched on the television. It was 2:45 P.M., his headache had returned, and because the NHK was rebroadcasting a boring debate in the National Diet, he decided not to listen, but just as he was reaching out to switch off the TV, an announcement from the Meteorological Agency interrupted the debate with a map and flashing earthquake alerts, a man's voice warning that powerful tremors were imminent and listing the affected prefectures: Miyagi, Iwate, Fukushima, Akita, Yamagata. Then the image of the parliamentarians returned as the voice said, "There's not much time left before it starts," and the National Diet Building began to shake; the image was lost. A studio presenter continued the broadcast. He gave safety instructions, then the studio in Tōkyō also began to shake, and shortly after that, the presenter reported an earthquake estimated at an intensity from 7 to 5, depending on the zone. At 2:50, five minutes after the initial tremor, a new warning came onto the screen, this time for a tsunami, for the northeast coastal area of Tōhoku, the Pacific coastal regions of Hokkaidō, and also Ibaraki, Chiba, and Izu Shotō. Keisuke, who had called two minutes earlier saying, "Nobu was supposed to be in Sendai," came and joined him. They watched the images of the earthquake in Tōkyō, and Keisuke tried unsuccessfully to reach his son—"The lines are overloaded," said Haru, "I'm sure he's fine"—then, shortly before four o'clock, the NHK showed images taken live from a helicopter flying over the mouth of the river Natori, to the north of Sendai airport. They watched in silence, and failed to understand what they were seeing. The news flashes filled the screen, relentlessly, chaotically: magnitude 7.1 on the Richter scale, epicenter in the Pacific ocean 130 kilometers east of Sendai, some damage to the nuclear power plant at Fukushima Daiichi, magnitude raised to 8, fires in Miyagi, an oil refinery ablaze in Ichihara, magnitude raised to who knew how much, residents less than three kilometers from the power plant ordered to evacuate—and still, unreal, impossible, obscene, the images of the tsunami clawing into the land. At six o'clock, Paul arrived at the warehouse, and Sayoko called. Her sister, who lived in the Kantō region to the south of Tōkyō, had just checked in, the family were all fine, she hoped Haru's apartment was, too. Nobu was on a field assignment in Sendai, he told her. There was a silence. "That's it," she said, her voice toneless, and Haru felt his stomach churn with fear. "I'll wait here for you," she added, and hung up.

There was no television in the house by the Kamo-gawa. Relieved they no longer had to see the images, they listened to the radio. Haru tried to reach some acquaintances in Sendai and Natori, to no avail. Keisuke lay on the floor, stretched out on the bare wood. Sayoko brought some strong tea and bowls of steaming rice, then, when she saw Haru looking up at her from under his eyebrows, she brought sake. Paul sat with his back against the maple tree cage, and they drank without knowing what they were doing. Sayoko came and went, mumbling off and on. At midnight, Paul left, saying he would return at dawn, Sayoko called to tell Shigeru that she would stay the night at Haru's, and the wake began, a wake with neither the dead nor a verdict, neither a body nor reality, in the evidence of tragedy and the desolation of fate—because all three of them were imagining Nobu's. But the following morning went by with no phone calls, while the news reports detailed ever increasing, ever more horrific casualties. Shortly before five in the afternoon, the NHK announced that there had been an explosion at Fukushima, and Keisuke chuckled.

"Here comes the atom. We're all here now, let the party begin."

"The cooling systems have shut down," said Paul. "The reactors will melt."

When the commentator read a reassuring press release from TEPCO, the utility running the power plant, Paul said, "The media will believe anything."

"Just the way they don't show any corpses," said Keisuke. "Did you know that I'm from Hiroshima, too? My father is from Kyōto, but my mother's from Hiroshima, and she went there for our birth. She waited for us with her mother and sisters for two weeks. Hiroshi and I were born on July 6, 1945, and she came back here on August 5, the day before the bomb. They all died. I've never been there."

The radio described the flooded power plant, with the cloud from the explosion towering over it.

"Nothing is less hidden than what is invisible," murmured Keisuke. "Lies, the atom—they're right there in front of us, in plain sight."

At seven o'clock, it was Paul's turn to murmur, "I feel as if I'm witnessing a collapse."

"Oh," said Keisuke, "we'll rebuild, at least partially. But you never knew Kōbe before Hanshin-Awaji. It was a young city, a special place, almost eccentric. We'll rebuild, but innocence— well, that's been lost forever."

At eight o'clock, Keisuke's telephone rang, and he handed it to Haru. It was Yukio, the biologist colleague with whom Nobu had been collecting samples on the shore at Shichigahama, twenty kilometers from Sendai. The *kami*, or the gods, or who knows who, had tossed one of the colleagues into his hotel room in the center of town to type up a report and the other onto the beach to gather his samples of sand. "The tsunami came after," said Yukio. "If he'd left right away, he'd still be alive. I tried to call him, but no calls were going through. I think he wanted to pick up all the equipment, got as far as the car, and then it was too late. It was swept away, to where I've just found it. It's a miracle, so many others won't ever find their loved ones"—he began to weep. Haru hung up, Sayoko went down on her knees and lowered her head, Paul clasped his hands behind his neck, devastated, desolate, and Keisuke looked at Haru.

"I told you," he said.

The urn was brought to the cemetery just after the funeral, which had been delayed by the identification and repatriation of the body. "Where will your ashes be?" Keisuke had asked Haru, adding, "Nobu deserves to have you as a neighbor." They met at Kurodani in the pouring rain, with a terrible sense of déjà vu. Hiroshi stepped up to say a prayer, then added a few personal memories, which caused Keisuke to collapse onto the sodden ground. Haru put down his umbrella, took his friend by the shoulders, and held him close until the end of the ceremony. Akira came over with another umbrella, but Haru waved him away and stayed there in the pouring rain, holding the brother of his heart. Then Paul closed his umbrella, too, and one by one all the mourners did likewise, letting their umbrellas fall behind them onto the muddy sand, openly accepting the rain and the cold air with the same affliction, in solidarity. When Beth closed hers, everyone could see that she was weeping. Sayoko's cheeks were streaming with tears and rain. She was the last to leave the path, her hair beaded with raindrops, her steps slow. A few days later, Paul asked Haru if Clara's ashes, too, could rest in Kurodani.

"She's a Buddhist," he said, "but even if she weren't, I'd want her to be there."

"Hiroshi will take care of it," Haru said, then lowered his voice, "Are we that close?"

"'We walk on the roof of hell, gazing at flowers,'" said Paul, quoting from a poem by Issa. "Really, we're already in the fiery furnace."

In the afternoon, Haru received the latest photographs from France and felt even more dejected. All those who could be happy were dying, those who were alive were unhappy, life was sinking into a swamp of misfortune and grief, and in that place he had run aground, as friend and father alike.

Information about March 11 continued to pour in. They learned that the earthquake had occurred at a shallow depth, that the plate movement had been concentrated along an unusually short fault line, building up energy in a confined space before giving rise to both a magnitude 9.1 quake and a monster tsunami. One evening, when Paul and Keisuke were at his place drinking sake, Haru shared his thoughts about the impossible depth of Japanese feelings.

"They exist," said Keisuke. "They're rich and fathomless, but we can't get at them. We're locked up in the misfortunes of our land, in its never-ending tragedy, and in our contemporary language, too, which can no longer express what we feel. How can we see into ourselves if we don't have the words for it? Instead, we get bombarded with disaster romanticism and the moral aesthetics of resilience. Oh, so admirable! But all they do is mask the desiccation of the modern soul."

The conversation continued along similar lines, in an atmosphere of sorrow and camaraderie.

In the end, Keisuke turned to Paul and said, "You've been rubbing off on us. Ordinary Japanese people don't like concepts. They prefer ritual."

"But all humans imagine life," said Paul.

"Life's a bitch," said Keisuke. "What more is there to say about it?"

Paul didn't reply.

"And you," Keisuke said, turning to Haru, "how do you see it?"

"Like a river crossing," he replied, "a river where the water runs so deep it is black. I can't see the bottom, but I still have to cross it."

Keisuke gave him an affectionate look.

"You're right," he said. "The dew is on the far shore."

In mid-April, Haru had lunch with Beth, who told him that from now on, she would be spending her summers in England.

"But you hate England," he said, surprised.

"Precisely," she said. "Japan eases my pain, but the drug is wearing off as the years go by. I need a bit of hell so I can find respite again. The business is doing well: I can run everything from my native Berkshire, and once I've had my fill of scones and sherry, I'll be back."

"When are you leaving?"

"After Clara," she said. "I'll come back in September; Paul will be glad to see a missing face."

That evening, Haru told Sayoko what Beth had decided.

"Let her stay there," she said.

He was stunned: he'd never heard her say an unkind word about anyone.

"She has no morals," Sayoko said, "and I don't just mean in her private life. Even in business there are rules. You can't just do whatever you like."

Not long afterward, Haru was on the phone with the client he'd been unable to visit the day before the Hanshin-Awaji earthquake. His daughter lived on the coast in the Miyagi prefecture. She'd survived the earthquake and tsunami, had taken refuge with her children at an emergency shelter, and then, when the roads reopened, made her way to her parents' place in Kōbe. "But the poor people who have nowhere to go are doomed to years of abandonment," he said to Haru. "Do you know who it was that came to the devastated areas just after the earthquake? It wasn't the government, local authorities, or foreign aid workers, who are all dependent on their equipment and their protocols and their inertia. The people who brought supplies and aid to the unfortunate, even in the radioactive zones, were the yakuza. In the early hours after the quake, the victims could only count on the Japanese people themselves and on the Inagawa-kai. If we're governed by bandits and rescued by other bandits, the most compassionate among them have every right to rebuild the country." And what about me, wondered Haru, am I a bandit, too? He put the question to Keisuke, who burst out laughing. "You are, but only a very minor one. Your racket's not that evil since your protégés get rich, and, moreover, you don't go around threatening people or bumping them off." "Neither does Beth," Haru pointed out, at which point Keisuke grew thoughtful and said, "No, but she's a vampire all the same." Some time later, they had another discussion.

"You're a businessman, but you're also a lover of beauty," Keisuke said. "That keeps you from being vulgar, as it does for Beth with her Zen raptures."

"Vulgar?" said Haru, recalling what his old master Jirō had said.

"But beyond pleasure, there's solitude," Keisuke went on. "You've always dreamt of elsewhere without ever going there, you wanted foreign women, you saw art as another place where you could lick your secret wounds. Your solitude makes you run away, but your wounds keep you grounded. And then, I sense that there's a redeeming factor in you, but I can't tell what it is."

C lara died on May 20 at the Second Red Cross Hospital. She was thirty-four years old. During the funeral, Paul could hardly stand, and Haru thought it was the saddest funeral he'd ever attended. The day they took the ashes to the cemetery, the weather was splendid. In the furnaces of hell, the ravens were squawking above the pathways, people's faces were caressed by a warm breeze, the graves hummed with the invisible life of the dead. Keisuke stood motionless throughout the service, as sober as a judge, his expression infinitely gentle. In the evening, he left to get drunk in town, and Haru went to Kamigamo with Beth. When they got there, Paul was making dinner for Anna, and his eyes, with their dark circles, broke their hearts all over again. Beth spoke Japanese to the little girl, who went into fits of giggles trying to say *daijōbu*. Clara's and Paul's parents, who were lodging at a nearby hotel, came and joined them, and Laura, who had stayed at home with the little girl during the ceremony, served the dinner that Sayoko had prepared and Kanto had delivered. At first, everyone spoke English, but when they realized that Beth's French was very good, they switched. Paul was a different man when he spoke his mother tongue, and Haru knew how much the presence of his parents and in-laws weighed upon him. "Laura is a gift from heaven," he'd said, "but I dread the arrival of the holy family, even if I know it's a good thing for Anna." He added that Clara had long thought that William died because he hadn't been able to inhabit his Japanese side, and she wanted Anna to know her Belgian side. Haru thought about his distant ancestors, observed Beth as she was making conversation, and wondered how intense her pain was now. On her right, Paul's father made him think of a bird of prey: straight, stern, with a stony gaze and imperious movements. At the end of the meal, he said something, and silence fell. Paul stood up and left the table, and everyone followed suit. Haru and Beth took their leave and went together into the night. "I'm going away," said Beth as they were parting. "I'm leaving for London tomorrow," and she gave the short, painful laugh he'd only ever heard in her darkest moments.

At midnight, Paul knocked at the door of the house by the Kamo-gawa.

"It's your fate to take in your grieving friends," he said.

He looked frightening.

"I'm grieving, too," Haru replied, and they went into his study.

"I thought I'd be consoled, knowing she's no longer in pain," said Paul, "and the thought is truly present, real and salutary. But it hasn't brought me any consolation."

They spent a moment drinking in silence before they spoke again, about everything, about Clara and Anna and love and, relentlessly, openly, about death.

"What was it your father said that made you all clear off?" Haru asked eventually.

"My father has a passion for judging rather than understanding," Paul replied. "He's one of those men who likes to prove he's always right."

A gust of cold air came in through the window. He didn't mind it, and shivered.

"But only death is always right," he murmured.

After Paul left, Haru wandered around the big room, smoking a few cigarettes, but just as he was getting ready for bed, he found, on the little table by the maple tree cage, the calligraphy of a poem with only one line, in Keisuke's hand.

Alone in the beyond reigns the dew

Then, just when everything was finished, everything continued.

It was during that time that the Japanese woman who'd been Haru's mistress in the early 1990s came back into his life. She'd just returned from another decade abroad with her diplomat husband, and Haru saw her again at an official reception in the salons of the Hotel Okura. "I'll be staying in Japan from now on," she told him, "Shohei will be in the Tōkyō offices for a while, and then he'll go overseas without me." "What are you doing in Kyōto?" he asked. She smiled and said nothing. She had just turned fifty. He found her beautiful, and changed. The next day they went to Shisen-dō, sat on the tatami in the temple gallery, and her hand brushed against his. "I'd like to bring Midori here one day," she said, and he remembered how she adored her only daughter. Large azalea petals, pinned against the tender green shoots of spring, painted a streak of pink stars. On the fine, flaxen sand there was an arrangement of ferns, hostas, heavenly bamboo, a stone, and a birdbath. In the background, a row of slender maple trees stood listlessly. The following day, Haru told Paul about his visit and at the last minute, without knowing why, refrained from mentioning Midori.

"The Shisen-dō? That's my favorite temple at this season," said Paul.

He leaned back in his chair.

"We walk on the roof of hell, gazing at flowers," he added.

With a calm and naturalness that surprised him, Emi became Haru's mistress once again. They saw each other in Kyōto and in Tōkyō, made love, conversed, laughed, went out to dinner. The hunger and tension of their first affair had given way to a tender, mischievous closeness, and bit by bit, Haru stopped seeing his other mistresses. Amid a flurry of tiny snowflakes, he celebrated his sixty-third birthday at the house by the Kamo-gawa. Emi featured prominently, and he noticed with amusement that in Sayoko and Keisuke she had found a silent sponsorship committee—and so, although he never spoke about private matters with Sayoko, the following day, he nonchalantly informed her that Emi was married. "As all we women are," she said with a shrug, and he laughed to himself to see her take a principle that she would ordinarily defend with her life, and throw it on the scrapheap. But he had to acknowledge that the life he'd been leading for forty years had been brushed aside, painlessly and without forewarning. He continued to go out, drink, do business, and party, but the spirit had changed. One afternoon, for the first time, he took Emi on his loop through the temples and cemeteries. They were alone, and she walked by his side, affectionate, elegant, and serious. At the top of the great stairway, they paused in the silence of the snow-covered city, in the deep calm of temples and graves. Haru looked at Emi, who was breathing lightly, on the verge of tears, she turned to him, and her eyes were shining. He admired her beauty and her delicacy. Then, turning his thoughts elsewhere, he mused to himself, Tomoo is still the form that gives my hill its spirit. Now is my time of mourning, and, from now on, it will be my dead who give these buildings and these tombs their scent of fervor. He stopped in the courtyard of the temple and saw again that early dawn of January 10, 1970, when Tomoo and Keisuke were walking ahead of him in the snow, and he felt himself shivering and being born. But Keisuke and Paul are alive and well, he thought, and Rose, too. A gong rang out, far in the distance, and he again became aware of Emi's presence.

In the evening they dined at a restaurant in Gion, an old establishment where Haru was an honored patron. During the meal, Emi told him about her years abroad, then about a love story she was reading, and, as he listened, he could envisage, as if he were at the theater, what his life would've been like had he married a Japanese woman. Just when he was thinking about how he'd always kept his desire well apart from his identity, Emi, still talking about the novel—the story of a married man and woman who end up committing suicide together—said to him, "My European friends think the Japanese have made a religion out of impossible love." The rest of the evening was spent in a muted atmosphere, where he felt like a dreamer passing through a landscape that was both familiar and strange. They walked through the freezing night to a wine bar, where Keisuke joined them. He was already quite drunk and started babbling with Emi. Haru listened distractedly and, before long, with an affectionate smile on his lips, stopped listening altogether. He sipped his glass of Chinon thinking about Rose, and told himself, I'm sitting here bored to make Emi happy; it would've been just like this, taking my daughter to a children's party.

On the morning of January 19, 2013, the day before Haru's sixty-fourth birthday, Sayoko paused abruptly by the picture window that looked out on the Kamo-gawa. "What are you looking at," Haru asked, and, puzzled, she said absentmindedly, "The river." At around seven that evening, Keisuke called him to suggest they meet Paul in town, but Haru had plans to spend the evening with Emi, and he declined. He met her at a sushi restaurant on the top floor of a building, and they ran into Beth there. She was back from England and was dining with business associates. They chatted for a moment, standing by her table. Later on, Emi said to Haru, "She's impressive, look how they respect her, even though she's a foreign woman," and Haru felt a whiff of nostalgia thinking about the bygone era when he and Beth were lovers. They had dinner, savoring the view onto the mountains of the East, then walked home along the Kamo-gawa. The weather was mild, and the wild grasses curved like arches of silver in the moonlight. At home, they took a bath and got into bed, chatting and laughing, but they didn't make love. Haru gazed at Emi's naked back and peacefully nodded off.

At six o'clock, his telephone rang, and he heard Keisuke's voice say, "Come to the Red Cross. We're more or less okay, but come." At the hospital, he found Keisuke in a corridor, disheveled and wearing hospital pajamas. "I'm not hurt," he said, "but I got thoroughly soaked," and then he told him what happened. They'd been drinking more than they should've—Haru could well imagine what that meant—and without really knowing how, they'd found themselves on the Sanjō bridge telling each other that they ought to jump in the river. They climbed over the railing, Paul struck the edge of a pillar, Keisuke landed in the cold water without too much damage, and they were immediately rescued. Paul had an emergency operation on his hip, and everything went well— "So to speak, that is," whispered Keisuke, "I'm such a moron. I know very well I can't die, but I should have protected him." "Where's Anna?" asked Haru. "With the babysitter," Keisuke said, "I called her just now, she was worried sick." Haru called Sayoko and told her briefly what had happened—"Ah!" she said. "The river!"—and told her to go to Paul's place. "I'll bring Anna home with me," she replied, and in the days that followed, Anna spent the day at Haru's and the night at Sayoko's while Paul slowly recovered. "I'll have a limp for the rest of my days," he told Haru, "but limping is the least of it. The truth is that I failed Anna, and I'll never forgive myself."

He did forgive himself. He started work again, found his way back into the bars, in moderation, and Haru loved to see him forging an affectionate and joyful relationship with his daughter. He had affairs, too, because he realized he could no longer be the man he'd been with Clara, that no man can measure up when facing the absence of the dead. When Haru saw that work kept Paul on his feet, he entrusted him with an ever-greater number of assignments, particularly as he knew the Japanese adored him. Paul drank valiantly during the endless dinners. He didn't say much, but he laughed and made others laugh at the right moment, and he concluded transactions, sometimes making an even greater profit than Haru might have done. When this made Haru laugh, Paul smiled and said, "The spirit of capitalism was born with the Protestant work ethic. I thought I loved art, but I'm merely a product of my culture."

But the truth was that he didn't smile often, and Haru felt sorry for him. Anna, who was four years old now, looked more like her mother every day, and despite absence and sadness, she seemed unfailingly cheerful and mischievous, which was why Sayoko was convinced the child was protected by the Tadasu forest. When Paul sold the house and moved to an apartment in the center of town, she was alarmed, and for a few months, she again kept a watchful eye on the little girl. But Anna was growing up harmoniously, and Paul drew his strength from this.

Haru celebrated his sixty-fifth birthday, and the party, jointly organized by Sayoko and Emi, was lovely. It was snowing, the lantern in its glass cage wore its immaculate raven's wings, and Keisuke gave a hilarious speech scattered with camellias, friendship, and sake, which ended with: "Mountain folk are real dumb-asses." Everyone laughed, and they headed into a delightful spring before the monsoon arrived early and, because it was unusually cold, Haru caught a chill. On the evening of June 29, he was at home drinking hot tea and trying to read despite the nasty cough that tore at his chest, when the new investigator called. The first one had retired ten years earlier, and his successor, who, like him, spoke English, apologized for calling without prior warning and then informed Haru that Maud Arden had committed suicide the day before.

S he had filled her pockets with stones and drowned in the river Vienne. Haru asked that reports on everything that happened be sent to him, and photographs arrived in his email inbox. He could see Paule in them, dressed in black, greeting visitors at the entrance to the sun room. One picture showed Rose leaving the apartment on the rue Delambre, her face hard and inscrutable: it reminded Haru of Maud's. The funeral service was held at the church in the neighboring town, and the deceased was buried in the same graveyard as her father, in the countryside ten minutes away. The photographer hadn't been able to get close; the pictures were blurry, and it was hard to make out faces, but it seemed to Haru that they wore pale masks, and like the actors in the Noh plays of his childhood, they were mixing with a society of ghosts.

"What are you going to do?" Paul asked the next day.

Haru coughed and lit a cigarette.

"I'll contact her, but I don't know how yet."

"And yet, 'how' is the Japanese question par excellence," said Paul. "I don't know any other nation that can brush aside the question 'why' so gracefully."

"She's always lived without a father and virtually without a mother," said Haru. "I can't suddenly pop up in her life, just like that."

He coughed again.

"You should see a doctor," said Paul. "You can't seem to shake that bronchitis."

"I'm going today. I have an appointment at four."

He walked to the doctor's along the Kamo-gawa, turning left onto the Demachi bridge and briefly going up Kawabata-dori. It was drizzling, he felt tired, and happy in an unimaginable way, something warm and deep, digging multiple wells of emotion in him. In France, the years had gone by in dreary repetitiveness. His daughter was declining, beautiful and morose, robbed of her anger, indifferent and, apparently, resigned. Almost nothing happened in her life anymore, she almost never saw her friends, had almost no lovers, just went to work and back home again, and whenever he received reports and photographs, Haru had to admit that Maud's black aura seemed to be winning. But now, very soon, Rose will come to know her Japanese soul, he thought, admiring the herons as they melted into the monsoon grayness. Along the edges of the riverbed, the wild grasses, green and plump with rain, bowed to the cool wind. Ahead of him, the mountains of the East formed a dark, secretive mass. All around, through the magic that combined contemporary blight and sanctuaries of grace, the dream of Kyōto entered him as never before, and he smiled as he thought, Wanting my daughter to become Japanese has made me more Japanese than ever.

Shigenori Mizubayashi, who had been Haru's friend for thirty years, chatted while examining him and, after a moment, fell silent.

"Have you lost weight recently?" he asked.

Haru had no idea.

"I'm going to send you for some tests," said Shigenori. "You're a heavy smoker, it's best to err on the side of caution."

"I don't have time to get sick," said Haru with a laugh.

He went for the tests and gave it no further thought, fully focused as he was on his Rose Strategy. Pleading his bronchitis, he declined Emi's offer to spend a few days with him, and he mostly stayed in his study, reflecting, while Paul took care of the business. On July 20, Shigenori called him and said, "I have the results of your tests. Can you come by this afternoon?" Haru looked at Sayoko, who was arranging lilac branches in a tall white vase, and, seeing that she was focused and serene, he didn't worry. He went on foot to the doctor's office on Kawabata, waited for a while, thinking about the first words he would write to his daughter, then Shigenori ushered him into his consulting room, and Haru knew at once that it was serious.

"Tell me straight," he said.

"We need to do a biopsy and other tests to find out more, but one thing is certain: you have cancer."

"Lung cancer?" Haru asked.

"Both lungs are affected."

"Now?"

The doctor looked at him, taken aback.

"Does it have to be now?" insisted Haru, and he gave that short laugh that he'd heard others give, thinking, This is how fate works.

"How bad is it?" he asked.

"We'll know better after the MRI and the biopsy," said Shigenori. "Don't take the news as a sentence. Lots of people live a long time with this type of cancer."

Haru went home, asked Sayoko to have tea with him, and broke the news. She ran his household, organized his schedule, and knew his secret: she of all people deserved to know what was going on. He was curious, too, to find out why the lady of tragedy had not gotten wind of this one, and he figured that perhaps this reflected a reason for hope. When he spoke to her, she gave a gasp of surprise.

"I don't believe it," she said, and he thought she was denying the reality of his disease.

He was wrong, because, anticipating his question, she added, "I'm always blind at home."

"At home?"

"I mean, here," she said, indicating the room flooded with light.

He underwent another series of tests and saw Shigenori in August.

"It's not the most aggressive, nor the most benign of cancers," said the doctor, "but there are very good treatments nowadays, and I'm going to send you to the best oncologist in Kyōto."

"How long have I got?" asked Haru.

"We don't know."

"How long?"

"Five years, maybe ten," said Shigenori, "but if we get you to your ninetieth birthday, don't take me to court."

Once he'd left the doctor's office, Haru called Paul and suggested they meet at Kitsune—"Sayoko will look after Anna," he said. "I need to have dinner with you." Paul arrived on time, sat down, let Haru order the beer, then said, "Tell me straight."

Once Haru had explained everything, he leaned back in his chair and said only, "I'm here."

"You're going to have to hold down the fort," said Haru. "No one likes merchants who are sick, and Japan in general doesn't like sick people. You'll represent us when I can't."

"Who else are you going to tell?"

"Keisuke, Beth, Emi, and once it becomes obvious, everyone."

The chef came to offer them a round of shōchū. Haru laughed and asked Paul if they looked that desperate. "We are desperate," the young man replied, and he smiled. They drank their shōchū in tall glasses with a lot of ice.

"My father died peacefully in his sleep," said Haru. "I'd almost convinced myself that I'd do likewise."

The evocation of his father made him drift toward other memories.

"I used to know a tea master in the mountains near Takayama. His name was Jirō Mifune; he had an antique shop in town, and in the middle of piles of junk, you could find treasures. He held court in his cabin, between crates of beer and stacks of old magazines, but I have never heard the call of tea more clearly than at his place."

He raised his glass to his invisible friend.

"He said that a man who thinks he knows himself is dangerous. But in fact, he followed the way of tea, and he knew who he was. I'm going to turn my little north-facing room into a tea room. I need to see, I no longer have the time to believe."

Paul raised his glass. "And Rose?"

Haru shook his head.

"I don't know yet."

T reatments, tests, weeks and months: all were cruel. In August 2014, Haru postponed his decision regarding Rose and, more generally, any meaningful decision at all. In June 2015, when the news on the cancer front was uncertain, he went with Kanto to the opening night of the Takigi-Noh festival. The weather was warm, slightly cloudy, and he was surprised to find himself enjoying the outdoor event, which reminded him of the performances of his childhood. When the torches were lit and the stage and shrine stood out against the background of expanding darkness, he was struck by the density that the real night conferred on the play. Beneath the rising moon, it made him see the world in a way he'd never seen it, and with an impression of wandering through secret provinces he nodded off, as if giving himself up to protective hands. And when he awoke, the lead actor was wearing the mask of an old man, which had certainly been sculpted by a great artist, because Haru had never seen such a vivid expression of pain. Or maybe I've just become more sensitive to it, he wondered, realizing with terror that this was the emaciated face of death, while the actor chanted, And if I am here, it is to tell you of my agony.

The following day, after a night of fractured sleep filled with dreams of drowning, of ghosts and demons, Haru organized everything without telling anyone. In the night lit with art and fire, he had seen the truth, and he knew, without needing a prognosis, that he did not have many luminous months left.

Three weeks later, he informed Paul and Sayoko that he would be going to Takayama for a few days, and he asked Kanto to come at dawn. At the break of day, he told him he'd like to be driven to Kansai International Airport, and would Kanto please not tell anyone. He watched the city streets rush by, then the suburbs, and then the plain of the South with, along the freeway, the horrible urban zone of Osaka. At the end of the drive the car crossed the great bridge connecting the airport to the coast, and he was amused to see the traffic signs in English and in katakana—the syllabary for transcribing foreign words—proclaiming, Sky Gate Bridge R. His gaze took in the great bay of Osaka, its industrial buildings, its fishing boats and cruise ships, its dreary concrete structures, and he could think of nothing more Japanese than this maritime landscape disfigured by modernity.

Kanto went with him to the check-in counter and the security line, then bowed and walked away as if he'd merely left his boss at the dentist's. After security and customs, Haru went to the business lounge and sat there in an armchair by the window looking out on the runways and the sea. One plane took off, another landed. He poured himself a coffee and went back to his armchair. He sat there for two hours before boarding, he picked up a newspaper, put it back down, more flights arrived, departed, the sea was getting rougher in the rising wind. He noticed that, depending on the phase of take-off or landing, the planes seemed alternately heavy or light, clumsy or graceful, and at one point the trajectory of a small plane made him think of the herons by his river and, by association, his childhood torrent. He recalled having seen the opposing shores of his life there and, in the middle of the flowing water, his daughter, enigmatic and sylphlike—This is where I am, he thought, so close to the molten heart of the mystery, in a place where I can be with Rose at last. The ballet of aircrafts continued, he drank two more coffees, nibbled some senbei, repeated to himself the name of the hotel he had booked in Paris. The sea was now a heavy swell beneath the inky clouds. He was afraid of the coming storm, but the departure board indicated the flights were on time, and he relaxed with a glass of wine. Finally, he left the lounge, the window, the sea, the runways varnished by the dark sky.

During the flight, it was impossible to sleep. The coffee, the length of the flight, the vagaries of travel: everything kept him awake. In the darkened cabin, his eyes open wide, he imagined the instant he would enter the same space as Rose and see her there before him, surrounded by the same air, coiled in the same web of existence. Once they landed, after twelve hours of this strange watchfulness, he was exhausted. As he left the arrivals hall, he saw his name on a sign held aloft by a Japanese man that Manabu Umebayashi had hired for him. He led Haru to a car, and Haru fell asleep almost instantly. When he awoke, they were already within Paris, it was early afternoon, and it was raining. The hotel seemed clean, the service mediocre, the room comfortable. He took a shower and lay on the bed, only regaining consciousness when it was pitch black outside. He slipped the telephone Manabu's man had provided for him into his pocket, and went out.

It had stopped raining, and he strolled aimlessly, keeping his bearings on the Tour Montparnasse. The city looked dirty and smelled bad. He walked for a long time through the sleeping streets, but he didn't care about Paris; he thought only about Rose. Before long, he got hungry. The day was dawning, and coming to a grand boulevard, he recognized the café. He had looked so closely at the photographs—those chairs of green and white wicker, the windows open onto the wooden counter, the waiters in their white shirts, black ties, and waistcoats. He found a table on the terrace and ordered breakfast.

Three decades of photographs had made Paris look familiar, but they did not convey the smells, the light, and, above all, the way people moved about. There at last, it was not so much the exotic nature of the setting, people's physiognomy, or the language, but the movement of passersby that immersed Haru in a bath of insurmountable strangeness. Meeting French people in Kyōto, spending time with Westerners—none of it had prepared him for this crowd with its specific gestures, and, drowning in this other-worldly tide, he felt removed from reality. After an hour, his fatigue got the better of him, and it seemed childish to have hoped for some miraculous appearance, so he thought about going back to his hotel to get ready for the following morning. His plan was to wait outside Rose's research institute just before she began work—he would spot her, and from that first impression, his subsequent decisions would arise.

He saw her coming straight toward him. She was crossing the boulevard, and he realized she was heading to her sidewalk café. She was wearing a very simple green dress and flat sandals, and her hair was loose. She looked at him without seeing him and sat at the next table. The waiter came over, she ordered a coffee, and the sound of her voice, in which he recognized his own mother's timber—the imprint of his mountains—staggered him. He was no more than three feet away from her, and as she was paying him no attention, he could study her at leisure. There was an energy about her that was not perceptible in the photographs and which, to Haru, evoked the fragile obstinacy of flowers. How many men have loved her for it, he wondered, and did they come up against her rage and indifference, too? As she raised her cup, she dropped her spoon on the ground. He picked it up and handed it to her. She thanked him, and he said, "You're welcome." She stared at him and hesitated.

"Are you Japanese?" she asked.

"Yes," he said. "Have you been to Japan?"

"No thanks," she answered, "not my cup of tea."

He smiled.

"We have beautiful things there, you know."

"Beautiful things?"

"Things may not be much," he said, "but still."

She ordered another coffee from the waiter as he walked by.

"What sort of beautiful things?" she asked.

"We have heavens," he said.

"Heavens?"

"Heavens where gardens wither, and where sometimes a fox slips by."

She gave him a hard look. "Do you have friends here?"

He detected a faint tension in her voice. He thought, It's coming now. Something clicked, opening a sort of breach in the web of things, through which he had the infinity of time to go inside himself before replying. A sudden torpor came over him there where he sat, and took him elsewhere, among the trees at Kokedera. He was wandering in the shelter of their foliage, was enchanted by their ability to give life despite their rootedness. He heard their song and understood the power of motionless transformation. He drifted for a moment close to the summits of memory, admiring the moss, the mists, letting himself go to the magical radiance of the earth. Truth flowed with the intermittent sparkling of the undergrowth, where he saw, in turn, the years, the solitude, the moments of helplessness. Soon he would be a burden to his loved ones, and, lulled by the leaves' lamenting, he thought, Nothing happens by chance. She was looking at him, he loved her with an impossible force, and, just like that, he tore his heart out.

"No," he said. "I don't know anyone in France."

She stared at him again, and shrugged.

"Of course," she said.

He thought of Beth and how the Nanzen-ji transformed her into another woman, and he reflected on his own fascination with elsewhere and how, here, he was simply a foreigner, and he reflected, finally, that to love was to give light. He spoke to her in Japanese. He told her she was a powerful flower, that he had faith in her strength and determination, adding that he hoped that, one day, spirit would reveal her heart to her. She narrowed her eyes, puzzled, called the waiter, paid for her coffee, and stood up.

"Have a nice time here," she said.

He followed her with his gaze as far as the entrance to the nearby metro, then he asked for the bill and went back to his hotel, following the directions on his telephone. He lay down on the bed. He'd been expecting an onset of intense, radiating pain, the kind that would leave him drained and charred, cleansed of emotion. Instead, he felt nothing.

He called the airlines and Manabu Umebayashi's man, had lunch and then dinner in his room, without going out. The next morning at dawn, his driver was waiting for him by the hotel entrance. This time, he wanted to experience every heartbeat from now until take-off, and he didn't sleep on the way to the airport. He checked his suitcase, went to the lounge, drank wine and coffee. When he took his seat on the plane, he prepared himself once more for a wave of sorrow, but, instead, what welled up inside him was a sense of dizzying relief and incomprehensible intoxication. The plane broke through the clouds, sunlight flooded the cabin, and he recalled Emi's novel about impossible love—impossible love which, like friendship, is a part of love.

Once Haru had returned to the house by the Kamo-gawa, he brought his broken father's heart back to life in the form of a dying man's heart, and he notified the living that he was now in an in-between realm where they could no longer reach him. The first to be informed of this migration without return was Emi.

"I can give you everything, but you don't want it," she said.

He gave her a look full of affection.

"I've spent happy years with you, but I'm a solitary man, and I can't share my illness with anyone."

"A solitary man?"

She gave a cynical laugh.

"A man who claims to know himself is dangerous," she said, and after holding him for a moment in her arms, she left.

In the evening, he joined Keisuke at a bar, told him what he had said to Emi, and added, "I know you'll blame me, I'm on the verge of doing so myself."

"What is a man?" asked Keisuke.

"You tell me."

"He is solitude, for a start."

"Precisely," said Haru.

"And then he is his fall, and his birth. You think you can be born alone?"

"On the contrary, it seems to me I'm going to die."

"Don't you get it? You who are always dreaming of elsewhere, you're so Japanese; we think we can control everything, but everything eludes us. Your obsession with form is an obsession with control. But at the heart of it is an abyss where we are blind, unless we agree to stop looking and let others show us who we are."

"I cannot ask this of Emi."

"You think you still have a choice! But every human being needs someone to accompany their fall and their birth."

Later, in the warm complicity of friendship, as the sake sweetened the air of dread, Keisuke started laughing.

"What an imbecile you are," he said, "and what a samurai."

The third person to be informed was Paul. Haru didn't tell him about Paris, only that he was giving up on the idea of ever knowing his daughter.

"But a father is a father, whether he's healthy or sick," said Paul, when Haru had finished speaking.

"An absent father who's become a sick father," said Haru.

"You have years ahead of you, and you want to give up on the most important meeting of your life?"

"All that lies ahead is disease, decline, and death."

He laughed.

"It's so easy to get it wrong when you don't have a knife at your throat, don't you think?" he said. "What a father must give his daughter is the knowledge that will enlighten her about herself. That's what Beth didn't know how to do with William: I owe Rose her Japanese side."

"And how do you hope to accomplish that at a distance?" asked Paul.

"I have a few years left to figure it out. It's strange—this decision has made death real to me, but I feel intoxicated and happy."

"It's the intoxication of giving," said Paul, "of giving without expecting anything in return, because you've grasped the true meaning of the gift. I envy you that feeling of elation."

But since the hours he'd spent in Paris, Haru knew it was the elation of deciding against the meeting and of knowing the paradox of an even stronger closeness because of it. The slow erosion of the certainty of knowing one another, which was what these last decades had been made of, was replaced by the promise of the only transformation that mattered, illuminated by those brief minutes of conversation with his daughter.

Summer and autumn went by in relative calm. The cancer was progressing slowly, neither retreating nor taking a dramatic turn for the worse, and Haru was able to lead an almost normal life, though he stopped smoking and drinking and knew every breath was numbered. In January 2016, he celebrated his sixty-seventh birthday in the house by the Kamo-gawa, which was bejeweled with a huge bouquet of white camellias. The black vase, matte and chalky, made a strong impression, and Keisuke, whose gift it was, agreed that it was a success. Young artists, too, were invited, which made the party joyful. They were proud to be there, unique and daring, just as Haru had been at their age, and there were lots of women, as usual. He found them lovely and luminous, he did not desire them but was glad of their presence and charmed by their talent—All I want now, he thought, watching them laugh and live, is closeness, the ultimate closeness with Rose, in spite of death.

It was during that time that winter covered the city with camellias and plum tree blossoms and the investigator informed Haru that Paule had passed away at the age of eighty-seven. She had died at home, in her sleep, without ever having been unwell, and Haru was so relieved for her sake, but so sad for his daughter's, that he didn't know what he really felt until he received the pictures of the funeral, of the cemetery, and of Rose, lost in a long black raincoat, standing tall in the rain, and alone, in spite of the crowd. Looking at the photographs with

Paul one evening in March, he realized that the rain looked black, and Paul, leaning over the picture, seemed troubled because, indeed, it was as if the picture had been streaked with fine dark scratches.

"Keisuke would remind you that due to the heat after the nuclear explosion, a black rain fell over Hiroshima and Nagasaki," said Haru, "a rain dark with ash and radioactive dust that cemented the atom to the ground and destroyed all hope."

That same evening, Keisuke came to dinner. Haru broke with his usual custom and drank a few cups of sake. They spent the evening in conversation, speaking of their dead, allowing life to glitter with its secret gems. In the end, Keisuke asked Haru whether, in his bedroom, he still had that painting he'd made as a young man.

"Would you like to see it again?" Haru asked.

"No, but did you know that it's a rose?"

Keisuke himself was surprised, and added, "I don't know why I'm telling you this."

He looked at Haru.

"But you know, don't you?" he said, and then he left.

By autumn 2019, the cancer had worsened, and Haru was exhausted by the treatment. He could no longer leave the house without oxygen, he had pain in his lungs and bones and took as little morphine as he could, but took it all the same. Sayoko called the shots now, organizing his life—nurses, care, the trips to and from the hospital—and eventually a hospital bed was moved into his room across from Keisuke's rose. Haru invited Keisuke to come over that day, and as he had done fifty years earlier, served tea in what was an unaffected but rather solemn ritual. He had arranged the little north-facing room for the tea ceremony, and in the tokonoma had placed a scroll featuring violets in the ice. He did everything else in the manner of his old master Jirō, performing the rite in no particular order as he conversed and savored in friendship the sweet madness of things. Naturally, sooner or later, they ended up in their favorite sparring match.

"You believe that spirit springs from form, but it's the other way around. Form is no more than the visible aspect of spirit and the perceptible fantasy of its mastery," said Keisuke.

"Which just goes to show that despite all your railing against religion, you're the more Buddhist of the two of us," said Haru.

"But which one of us is more Japanese?" said Keisuke.

In May, the month of revelations, of beginnings and endings, Haru had a dream: he was walking with Rose along the pathways at the Kitano shrine. She was the embodiment of the woman he had met in Paris, a woman the photographs had failed to recreate for him. Standing before an iris of extreme beauty, he held out his hand to her and said, You will risk the unknown, suffering, giving, love, failure, and transformation. And so, just as the flower has passed into me, my entire life will pass into you. He awoke to intense pain; a few months earlier, he had decided that pain like this would seal his final decision. He took just enough morphine to get up and telephone Paul, who came after the first nurse had left. They drank their tea by the maple tree cage, and Haru explained that soon he would no longer be able to leave his bed, or remain conscious, or even swallow, and that consequently the time had come. As Paul didn't say anything, he added that he wanted to die at home, in Shinnyo-dō, that he had arranged everything with Hiroshi, and that he would breathe his last in a little garden adjacent to Hiroshi's private quarters. "You're going to commit suicide in a temple?" asked Paul, stunned. "I'm going to go to sleep there," he said, "Keisuke and you will bring me back here for the finale." "Hiroshi knows about this?" "Of course he doesn't," Haru replied, then added, "But first, I have to ask you to translate a letter and write down an itinerary.

"For Rose," he concluded. "Do you remember what you said to me, that first time in Takayama? How the depth of the Japanese soul is just below the surface, that our gardens are its substance taken form, so that hell might become beauty? For a long time, I thought Rose's sadness only had to do with Maud, I didn't want to see the aspect of hell we mortals are made of."

He laughed.

"Now, I want to leave Rose her Japanese heritage: more sadness, but with an indication to its antidote. I had an intuition about it in Kokedera eight years ago, and now I know that what I must give my daughter will consist of a letter and an excursion. When she comes to Kyōto to hear my will, you'll take her to a few chosen spots. At the end, you'll go with her to the lawyer's, then you'll give her my letter and its translation into French."

Paul didn't say anything, but Haru knew that his silence implied consent.

"I'm leaving her everything I own, but the company and the warehouse will be yours."

"That's out of the question," said Paul. "I'm not your son, and I'm not just your employee anymore. I'm also, and above all, your friend."

Haru nodded his head.

"When?" asked Paul.

"May 20, ten days from now."

And so Haru let himself sink into the limbo of his imminent death. To carve out the work, he invited Keisuke over for their last tea, and there in the half-light of the little room, he told his friend.

"Those who want to die go on living, those who want to live take their own lives," whispered Keisuke. "I've often tried, but who's a match for fate? It punishes us indiscriminately, loners and lovers, all of us deprived of communion with ourselves and our loved ones. And as for me, I'm the poor guy who keeps watch and chronicles the story, right down to its last word."

"Story? But whose story?" asked Haru.

"Who knows? I'll find out when my turn comes around. Maybe I'll be next? Or after Paul? I hope not. I'm old, and I want him to love again and to live for a long time."

Haru poured the tea, his movements gentle, slowed by illness and memories, blessed by the shade of his old master, by his native mountains, his torrents, his magical foxes. They drank without speaking, seated without ceremony, and the shadows descended in large numbers from his memory and its slopes, and a thickness of twilight crept over him. As Keisuke smiled at him, he reminded him of the story about the fox at Kakurezato and how, forty years earlier, it had crossed an invisible ford, then the story of the fox and the lady from Heian.

"One day, forty years ago, I told that story to a Frenchwoman," he added, "and then to Jacques Melland. Both of them were marked by it, but I never found out why."

Keisuke gave a chuckle.

"The fox says whatever you want him to say. In every good story, there are three main lines that meet, where we poor specks of dust move about, and where each of us shoves our life along according to our individual resources and weaknesses. Birth, love, and death. The original tale, the beginning and the end."

He lit a cigarette.

"I remember the Frenchwoman," he said. "In her case, I would have continued the story like this: in that life confined by invisibility where the reclusive lady lay dying, the fox's gaze caused the borders to flicker. That gaze provided her with unfamiliar mirrors, and altered the laws of intimate refraction. It arranged the shadows according to a new choreography. Eventually, it gave birth, for the lady, to another world, also invisible, where the heart of her life became visible, and by naming the dead, it set her free from their chains. The fox was the only friend she would ever have, the friend who, for her, would testify to her bereavement, subdue the shadows, and tame the invisible."

He looked pensively at Haru.

"You do know she was crazy, don't you? Crazy, inconsolable, or captive, call it what you like."

He crushed out his cigarette.

"But you're not telling me everything."

Haru gave him a smile.

"You'll know everything," he said.

Sayoko came in, the afternoon continued on its painful path, and Haru didn't give their conversation any further thought. But later, as he pressed the controls of his bed to lie flat, he wondered, If tea makes you see the invisible, what am I seeing? And then he had a vague intuition and thought, The fox is the key.

BIRTH

In the hour of his death, Haru Ueno thought: Now I see, now I'm in accordance with things. He gazed at the black bowl and welcomed its presence, a pure form without form, through which he now understood Keisuke. He gazed inside himself at an iris, and in this flower that had become his own, the pain lifted.

He thought: I've found my story, the one that consoles me and keeps suffering at bay. I thought I was giving it to others, but in truth, I was telling it to myself. To Melland, the fox said, Everything that has not been fervent will be erased; misery and grace are equally infinite. To me, it said, Every human walks toward the hour of their birth; we die into solitude and are reborn into light. Thus, the true journey is in the interval between this end and this illumination.

He thought: Rose, everything has been sorted, all that's left are the bare bones of existence, and I know that nothing in my life has been stronger or more important than you have. I'm the Japanese man who will have been the father of a French child, the depths of my soul are in that divide, it makes up my dark and sparkling legacy, my legacy of ancestors and estrangement, of solitude and closeness, of melancholy and joy.

Finally, while the dew from another shore beaded the garden in Shinnyo-dō, Haru Ueno thought: The dead are superior to the living, for their fall has ended at last.

ACKNOWLEDGMENTS AND THANKS
TO

Eva Chanet and Bertrand Py
Richard Collasse, Hiroko Ito, Corinne Quentin
Shigenori Shibata
and, as always, Jean-Baptiste Del Amo

About the Author

Muriel Barbery's novels include the *New York Times* bestseller, *The Elegance of the Hedgehog* (Europa, 2008), *Gourmet Rhapsody* (Europa, 2009), and *A Single Rose* (Europa, 2021). She is also the author of *The Writer's Cats*, illustrated by Maria Guitart, *A Strange Country*, and *The Life of Elves*. Barbery has lived in Kyōto, Amsterdam, and Paris, and now lives in the French countryside.